KT-526-786

This Northern Sky

JULIA GREEN

BLOOMSBURY

LONDON NEW DELHI NEW YORK SYDNEY

For Jesse and Jack
With love

Bloomsbury Publishing, London, New Delhi, New York and Sydney

First published in Great Britain in July 2013 by Bloomsbury
Publishing Plc 50 Bedford Square, London WC1B 3DP

A CIP catalogue record for this book is available from the British Library

ISBN 978 1 4088 2069 8

Typeset by Hewer Text UK Ltd, Edinburgh
Printed and bound in Great Britain by CPI
Group (UK) Ltd Croydon CR0 4YY

1 3 5 7 9 10 8 6 4 2

www.bloomsbury.com

The Shipping Forecast

Rockall, Malin, Hebrides, Bailey
Wind southwesterly 5 to 7,
becoming cyclonic 6 to gale 8 later;
severe gale 9 later.
Sea state moderate,
becoming rough or very rough later.
Showers then rain.
Visibility moderate,
occasionally poor.

I'm thinking about this photograph Sam showed me. We were round at his nan's after school. I'd been worrying about stuff – my parents, as usual. All their arguing, and the silences, which were worse. Sam used to listen, kind of, while I went on about it.

But right now, this particular afternoon in May, he was totally mesmerised by the picture he'd Googled. It was a photo of Earth, taken from the spacecraft Voyager, 3.7 billion miles away: the furthest away point *ever* that a photo's been taken of our planet.

'That tiny blue dot is where *we* live,' Sam said. 'Where all the people who have *ever* lived have spent their entire lives. It's smaller than a speck of dust in sunlight.' He looked at me. 'What does that make you think, Kate?'

I peered at the picture again. The Earth was just a distant spot, absolutely *tiny*, caught in a ray of light, and around it was space: dark nothing, stretching for ever. 'I suppose it shows how small and insignificant we are. Like nothing we do or don't do is so important, in the grand scheme of things.' I smiled back at him. 'So maybe I shouldn't worry about things so much. Is that what you mean?'

Sam sighed. It wasn't what he wanted me to say, obviously. He carried on scrolling down the screen, reading the text, checking out photos as if I wasn't there at all. And it was time for me to go home by then, in any case. He was about to have a driving lesson – paid for by his nan, even though she hardly had any money. But she didn't want him getting a job. *Not while you're studying. This is your big opportunity, Sam. You're the first one in this family with a chance of going to university . . .*

So, thinking about it now, perhaps Sam was simply imagining himself in the spacecraft, with that view of the spinning world from far off in space. He was going to be an astronaut, or some kind of astrophysicist, just as soon as he could get away. If he could hang on long enough at school to get his exams. If he could stop himself doing something random and crazy. If he could get the money.

If if if.

One

We've been on this train for hours: Mum, Dad and me. Each hour takes me further from home. After everything that's happened, you'd think I'd be glad about that, but I'm not. I'm hot, and tired, and I'm trying not to think about Sam, and the mess he *did* make, after all.

I've got the window seat, at least. The train flashes past hundreds of small scenes: freeze-frames from other people's lives. Two kids on a bridge over a river – a park with swings – a toddler in a pushchair holding a balloon. Chimneys – canal – motorway – row after row of brick terraced houses. A party in a sunny back garden – a gang of boys on bikes doing wheelies on a building site . . .

It all changes again. Now there are just fields: mile after mile of green, and acres of sky.

Pine forests.

Bare hills.

Moorland.

Sheep.

Tall pink flowers grow like spears along the railway embankment. Thistledown wafts in the draught from the speeding train.

The train slows down. Signals, I presume. We wait for ages in the middle of nowhere. I stare at a small white house tucked under the bulk of a smooth green hill. With four windows and a door in the middle and chimneys at each end of the tiled roof, it's like a storybook house, from when I was little and Dad read to me at bedtime and things were happy and uncomplicated. A long time ago.

We pick up speed again. On and on and on.

The crowded train begins to empty out at each station.

Mum falls asleep in the seat opposite me. Her head lolls against Dad's shoulder and he shifts away slightly. He's been reading the whole way. There's this horrible tense silence between them. We haven't left that behind, then.

I think about what Mum said to make me come with them, and the way her voice faltered, as if she was going to cry. *This might be the last time. Please, Kate. For my sake, and Dad's. We really, really need this holiday. Perhaps if I can get Dad away from work and everything . . .*

My head aches. Too hot. I lean it against the cool of the glass, but the window shakes too much for me to rest there for long.

The sky gets darker, the shadows lengthen.

Still the train rushes on.

There's a brief flurry of activity when we have to

6

change trains at Glasgow, on to a smaller one. Mum's anxious we're going to miss the connection: it's the last train this evening. There won't be another till the morning. Dad's obviously irritated with her, but he doesn't say much to me except *hurry up, keep up.* I trail behind them across the busy station concourse, weaving between people, my stupid bag bumping along on its clapped-out wheels.

The train's waiting. We've got booked seats, but it's not crowded like the last one. The two carriages rattle up the valley next to a loch for miles and miles. It's late, but there is still light in the sky, enough to see by.

Finally we're at the end of the line. We get off and join a huddle of people making their way to the ferry terminal. I veer off, to walk to the end of the pier next to the terminal building. Lights stretch out in wiggly lines over the dark water. It's blowing a gale.

Mum comes after me. 'Pull your hood up, Kate, for goodness' sake! Or take my scarf.'

I don't say anything.

'And please come back in a minute and wait inside, like everyone else.' She hurries back to the brick building at the edge of the car park.

We've been travelling all day and we're still not there yet.

The men on the ferry shout to each other, coil huge ropes, hose down the deck. Finally everything's ready. They let the cars on first, then the foot passengers. I wait till the very last minute before I turn back and join my parents at the back of the queue.

Dad's furious. 'Why do you always have to go off at exactly the wrong moment?'

'So?' I say. 'I'm here now, aren't I? What's the problem, exactly?'

'Stop it, both of you,' Mum says. 'Everyone's tired; let's all make an effort. Please.'

We dump our luggage in the special compartment on the middle deck. I go up the stairs and outside on to the deck at the back of the ferry. The horn blasts out and there's a stink of engine diesel. The ferry swings out across the water. I stand right at the edge, leaning over the rail. If you fell off, no one would know. The wind is like ice, and this is high summer.

Mum again. 'Come and sit down in the warm, Kate. There's another three hours at least. You're making me nervous, doing that.'

The water is deep and dark. It shines like treacle in the lights from the boat. You'd go down, down, down.

Mum gives up on me and goes back inside. I watch her and Dad through the window. At least they're talking, now, even if it is about me. Mum gets up and goes to the bar. Dad opens his book again.

Black water.

Grey-black sky.

The ferry creaks and sighs. On the car deck below, the cars and vans slide and clank as the ferry ploughs on, out across the open sea.

Dark shapes loom against the grey – other islands.

Every so often, a tiny light winks out into the darkness.

*   *   *

The crossing takes hours. Finally the low shape of the island looms ahead; Mum points out a white house on a headland. The engine roars as the ferry slows down and turns to reverse into position to dock. We stumble off down the gangplank once the cars have disembarked. A taxi's waiting for us. Dad helps the man load our bags into the boot. Mum slides into the back seat and leans over to hold the door open while I climb in.

The taxi man says something to Mum but his accent is so strong I can't understand a word. I could die from tiredness.

'Yes, four weeks. Lucky us,' Mum says back. 'It's good to be here again. It's been a long time.'

Dad watches the road ahead intently. The man's driving too fast: Dad's having to stop himself saying something. I know because of the way he's hunched up and silent, and because I can't bear it either. I'm thinking of Sam, of course, and that horrible night, the glare of lights . . .

Here, there are no street lights, no houses or anything. Rain spatters against the windows like handfuls of gravel. We rattle over a cattle grid and the taxi slows down and veers off to the right, on to a bumpy track. It stops. The engine's still running. He piles the luggage on to the grass and is off again the minute Dad's paid him.

We stand there a moment, all three of us, watching the red tail lights fade and disappear into the night. There's this rushing sound, like white noise.

The sound of nothing.

'Well, this is it,' Mum says. 'We've arrived.'

Dad picks up two of the bags, Mum opens the unlocked door. She has to shove it with her whole body. 'Wood's warped,' Dad says. 'Damp.'

I follow them in.

'Choose either room upstairs,' Mum says to me. 'We'll take the double room downstairs, won't we?' She glances at Dad, only for a second, fleetingly, but I notice all the same. Something flickers across his face too. He doesn't say anything. In the electric light his face looks washed out.

I stand at the top of the stairs to examine the rooms. Each has a sloping roof, Velux skylight windows, bare wooden floor with a sheepskin rug, a single bed, a chair, a chest of drawers and a shelf for books. I choose the one at the front, with an extra low window you can see straight through when you lie down on the bed. It's a square of black right now.

It's the middle of the night. I kick off my shoes, undress and climb under the duvet. Voices drift upstairs: a kettle flicks on; a door closes.

Something wakes me and for a moment I have no idea where I am. Strange silver light floods the small room, shines right on my pillow, on my face. There are two skylight windows, and one of them frames a full moon.

That moonlight! I've never seen anything like it. Shining right in, directly on me, like a spotlight. As if it means something.

I'm wired: too anxious, too awake, even though I'm so tired. I lie in the moonlight, listening to all the sounds of a strange house. That rushing noise is still there. The wind's up: it rattles the windows, shakes the house. I feel weird, as if my body's still travelling, up and down like the rocking of the train, the boat.

The moonlight moves across the room, off my pillow.

I make myself breathe deeply but I'm all on edge. I stay like that for ages. The moon moves across the sky. The room gets darker. It begins to rain again. Finally I fall into ragged sleep.

TWO

Morning. I wake up earlier than usual because it's so light. Not moonlight filling the square of window now but sun, and a blue sky with big clouds. From the bed I can see straight out of the low window: a square of sea and beach, framed by the window like a picture. The beach is really close: just a few metres in front of the house beyond the grass and the track.

Slowly it dawns on me that the sound I've been hearing all night, the rushing sound when we got out of the taxi, is the sound of the sea. Waves, rolling in, one after another. Watching them makes my head spin after a while, because it's never-ending. It's rough today – white-capped waves all the way out to the horizon.

I get up and go downstairs, use the bathroom, check the fridge but it's empty except for a carton of milk and some leftover cheese sandwiches from the journey, all squashed and disgusting. No one's up yet: Mum and Dad's bedroom door is shut. I listen: no raised voices. No sounds at all. I open all the kitchen cupboards and find tea bags and tins of soup and a bag of dry oats but that's about it. I make tea to take upstairs with me.

My room is so light and bright I'll never get back to sleep. I get dressed instead: jeans, T-shirt, jumper. It's bound to be cold outside. I check my phone but there's no signal. I stuff it in my pocket. I'll walk till I find a place where it works.

The wind's stronger than I expect: it whips the door back and makes it bang. Three sheep stop and stare at me as I walk over the grass to the track: there are sheep everywhere, not fenced in or anything, wandering all over the road and the grass. They run away, bleating, as I get near.

The track runs down to the road, and beyond that is the sea. The road follows the curve of the island. The tide's going out, revealing sand, wet pebbles, heaps of seaweed.

I jump down on to the nearest bit of beach. My feet sink in the sand. White, fine sand made of ground shells. I leave a trail of footprints: the first ones on clean washed sand. Like being the first person to walk on fresh snow. I pull my hood up and walk further along. Little brown birds fly off in front of me.

Phone's still not got a signal.

Now what? It's too cold to stay outside, and I'm starving.

I walk back towards the house. It's harder work, against the wind. Facing this way I can see the cluster of white houses which is the village. Except it's not really. There's only one shop, still shut. Sheep. And that's it.

The way Mum talked, you'd think it was going to be some kind of island paradise. She and Dad had their honeymoon here. Lots of holidays before I was born, when my sisters were little, and some when I was there too, apparently, and we were all *so happy* . . .

One last go, she said to Dad, the night before we left. *If we can't make things work there, we'll know that's it. The end of the line.* I wasn't supposed to hear, but the living room door was open and I was standing at the top of the stairs and I couldn't help it, and now the horrible words are stuck in my head for ever . . .

I pick up a handful of damp pebbles from the beach and fling them so they spray against the road. I yell into the wind.

A red post van goes by. The bloke driving it waves at me and grins. Like he thinks he knows me, or something. Like it's normal to be yelling and throwing stuff before breakfast.

I turn away. *Stupid. Stupid. Stupid.*

The wind makes my eyes sting with tears.

Dad's found a pair of binoculars and he's staring out of the window with them. Mum's making breakfast. 'Porridge,' she says. 'Want some?'

'What else is there?' I say.

'Nothing, I'm afraid. The shop won't be open yet,

so we're having to make do for now.' She glances nervously at Dad, as if she feels bad about there being nothing nicer for their first holiday breakfast, as if it's all her fault or something. I can't stand that. So I make an effort and eat her porridge and don't moan.

'What's it like out?' Mum says, with that hopeful look she has when she's trying to make things OK. 'Nice to have an early walk.'

'It's freezing,' I say. 'My phone doesn't work.'

Mum laughs. 'Well, that's one of the things I love about this place. No phones, no internet. Being cut off from all that.'

'It's not funny!' I say. 'How am I supposed to talk to my friends? Why didn't you say about that before we came?'

But I don't want to argue with her, I really don't. So I shut up and have another cup of tea.

Dad's checking his own phone.

Mum watches him, anxious. She doesn't say anything for a while. She washes the bowls and mugs and I wipe the table.

'We'll get sorted out this morning: get some food in and make ourselves comfortable in the house,' Mum says. 'Later let's go out together and explore this side of the island. I fancy a long walk along a beach. The weather's clearing, I think.'

Dad's staring out of the window. Why doesn't he say something nice to Mum? Say anything, for that matter? It's as if he's always thinking about something else.

The clouds have lifted. Now I can see a whole new layer to the view that wasn't visible before: other islands, one behind another, faint on the horizon.

At least the house is OK, I suppose. You could lie on the leather sofa and stare at the view and read and watch telly and stuff. There are DVDs and a pile of magazines and shelves of books, like someone's proper home instead of a holiday house. But four weeks, on a tiny island, with Mum and Dad trying to save their marriage and nothing, absolutely nothing, for me to do?

'I can't believe you made me come here!' I blurt out.

Dad looks at me. 'What else did you expect us to do?' he says. 'We were hardly going to leave you behind all by yourself for four weeks. You're fifteen, Kate. You're still a child. And after all the – the terrible business with that boy –'

'Stop right there!' Mum says, more fiercely than I've heard her for ages. 'Don't drag that up now.'

They mean Sam, of course. *Unsuitable* Sam with his brilliant mind and reckless behaviour: too old for me, too complicated, too dangerous. *You could have died*, Dad said. *How could we ever trust him, after that? How could you?*

In any case, Sam will hardly be desperate to see me, will he? Not with me being a witness and everything . . . So Mum and Dad needn't worry any more. Not about me, at least.

'You go for your stupid walk,' I say. 'I'm not coming.'

*   *   *

16

But I do go out, later. I walk away from the village down the single-track road and come across a huge beach of white sand with a fringe of grey-green grass. I walk along the sand, and after a while I find this rock shaped like a kind of bowl, big enough to lie in. It's the perfect shape and size so I can stretch right out, my head held by the curve of stone, my feet resting on the bottom lip. The rock is warm from the sun. I lie there, cradled in stone, trying not to think too much about Mum and Dad, all the stuff going on. The words they don't say. The undercurrents of anger and the clipped conversations and the way they look at each other.

Suppose this really is the last holiday we have together?

I let my mind drift off in all the space and light. I have never seen so much sky. The tide's coming in. Waves splash on the rocks further down, tug and grind and pound, a rhythm of sound. I close my eyes.

It might be OK, the waves say, and my heartbeat steadies at last.

I take a deep breath in.

Let it out.

Repeat.

I stay there for ages, eyes shut.

Perhaps I actually do go to sleep. Something makes me jolt – as if I'm falling. A new sound, not waves or wind or seabirds – a pattern of feet on sand and rock. I open my eyes. A boy – about sixteen or seventeen – is running along the shore. He doesn't see me. He's

17

playing some sort of game, it looks like: he hops, left foot, right foot, both feet together. He misses his footing for a second, slips, and pebbles spill and scatter from his pockets: a clatter of stone on stone. He laughs, picks up the pebbles and stuffs them back in his jeans' pockets, runs on.

Once he's disappeared round the curve of the bay, I ease myself out of my stone bed. My legs are stiff from lying still for so long. I cross the strip of grass and wild flowers at the top of the beach, start walking back towards the house.

Almost there.

Mum and Dad are standing side by side in the small front garden. They're not touching. Not speaking either. You could fit a third person in the space between them.

Mum's seen me. She waves.

Dad puts his hands in his pockets, goes back into the house.

Have they been arguing again? I can't tell from here.

Mum walks the short distance to meet me.

'Isn't it lovely?' she says. 'Is it coming back to you now? Did you remember the beach?'

'Not really,' I say. The truth is, I don't remember any of it.

Mum sighs. 'All those wonderful summers when you were little and we were so happy all together, but you don't remember?'

'Bonnie and Hannah do,' I say. 'They were that much older.'

Mum looks sad. 'And yet neither of them would come this time.'

'They're busy with their own lives now,' I say. 'You know that.'

'Well,' Mum says too brightly. 'Dad's been to the one and only shop already and stocked up. He's making supper tonight. He insisted.'

My mind flips into overdrive again. Dad – cooking and shopping? Anyone else would think how lovely, how kind: Dad's making an effort. But I've already clocked the fact that next to the shop is a public telephone box. In my mind, I see Dad talking softly into the mouthpiece of the old-fashioned phone in the red kiosk, half turning to check no one is watching him. It's like a scene in a bad film on telly: the stupid clichéd image of an affair.

I don't know any of this for sure.

I'm just guessing.

I'm not supposed to take sides, Bonnie says. Mum and Dad both love us; it's not about *us*.

Mum and I stop at the gate and we both turn at the same time towards the sea.

We just stand there for a while without saying anything.

'It won't get properly dark till really late, and in hardly any time at all it will be dawn again,' Mum says, 'because we are so far north.'

The air feels cool and thin. We're a very long way from home. For a second, I like this sense of being at an edge, remote and out of reach. It keeps Dad safe, and away from anyone else; closer to Mum. Maybe

Mum's right. Maybe that is all that's needed. Four weeks of them being together, no one getting in the way. I can leave them to it . . .

Except, what am I going to do?

A flock of black and white birds fly low across the bay making a high piping sound. That boy is coming back along the top of the beach. He looks up and waves as if he knows us and keeps on running.

Mum waves back. 'He'll be one of the lads from the Manse, I expect,' she says to me. 'The big house we saw as the ferry came in, that used to belong to the church.'

'What, he lives there?'

'Only in the holidays. He'll be away at school in England somewhere, I imagine, like his brothers used to be. Twin boys, Bonnie's age, I think. Funny, I'd forgotten all about them. But he looks just like one of the twins.'

I can't imagine anyone choosing to live here for real: it's so far from the mainland, so difficult to get to. All that's here is a few houses, and farms, I suppose, seeing as there are sheep and cows wandering all over the place. Beaches, yes, but nothing else.

Mum's still talking. 'They used to have house-parties at the Manse. Their rich friends came and stayed all summer. It looked such fun . . . you know, lots of games on the beach and barbecues and boats and things like that.'

I watch the boy as he runs on. He looks OK. I think of Sam, back home. *Not now, don't think about him now.* But the ache in my heart won't go away so easily.

20

Three

I am Kate, named for my grandmother who died just before I was born, which meant that when I was a newborn baby Mum was still grieving for her own mother. Mum likes to tell me that my grandmother, Kate, did see me once, kind of: the small, grainy photograph taken at the thirteen-week scan of me as a tiny foetus inside Mum's womb. *So she knew about you, and was happy that you were on your way, and she would have loved you very deeply.*

I am small and dark-haired like my grandmother in the old photos of her, and like Mum too, whereas my sisters, Bonnie and Hannah, are both fair and tall like Dad. They are five and seven years older than me: I was the surprise baby.

Every birthday I have, Mum thinks about Grandma and remembers her death all over again. She says it often happens in families, that there's a death and a birth very close together, *as if one soul makes room for the other. Or as if . . .* and she looks at me, *as if . . .*

As if what? The soul of my grandmother is reborn in me, or something? That's a weird thought. Like recycling people. Dad has this phrase: what goes around comes around. I suppose it's like believing in reincarnation and karma: you might come back as an insect or a bird or something worse. But *I* think I am uniquely me, not a version of my grandma, or anyone else for that matter. Newly arrived when I was first made. When I die, I'll disappear for ever, not be reborn in a different body. That's what I think.

There is going to be a lot of time for thinking on the island. Too much. I'm writing things down in the notebook Dad gave me on my birthday. My thoughts come out quite randomly sometimes. Like one idea runs into another and then they both skip off somewhere unexpected, and I have to pull them back and make them be sensible and stay on the lines. (There aren't any lines really: it's a notebook with creamy blank pages, and a copper, black and gold hardback cover, very beautiful. Dad knows how to choose stationery at least).

I decided that I would write down everything that happens in this, my sixteenth summer, at least until the pages run out. Today is July 27th, but I'm not going to put all the dates. I have even given it a title: *The Story of My Heart*. It's borrowed from a real book, one with a leather binding and old-fashioned print, which lives on a shelf in Dad's office. I haven't read it or anything: I just like the title. I like the feeling of writing things down too. It anchors me, this act of writing, and makes me feel more substantial and real, part of things. Especially now, with everything falling apart. It stops me from feeling as if I'm nothing and nobody, as if I might simply be blown away by the wind.

Almost dark: the sky through the skylight window is a thin blue-grey. Wind rattles the frame. It's starting to get at me, that wind. It never gives up. Now I'm lying down I've got that rocking feeling again as if I'm still travelling, bobbing up and down on water.

Dad is reading downstairs, Mum went to bed ages ago. I don't understand why she doesn't make at least a bit of an effort. Even at supper she seemed quiet and distracted, as if her mind was elsewhere. Dad had cooked lamb chops and new potatoes and beans and there were raspberries and cream for pudding and she didn't say anything at all about how nice it was.

Someone – Mum? – has put a pile of books on the shelf by my bed – nothing I want to read – plus a load of random DVDs. I scan the titles. *Deep Blue*; *Juno*; *Into the Wild*, *Cinema Paradiso*, *Fargo*; *My Summer of Love*. On the other shelf there's a collection of pebbles and fragments of polished sea glass: blue, amber, green.

I remember that boy from the Manse. Maybe I'll walk over there in the morning.

Just to see what the house is like.

Just because it's something to do, that's all.

Four

Mum and Dad are having some sort of horrible row downstairs. It's been going on and on for hours, it seems. Shouting first, and then quiet sobbing, and now raised voices I can hear even with the pillow wrapped round my ears. Words fly out like sparks.

No!

Why not?

Trust . . .

Unbearable.

I stand on the bed so I can push open the skylight and let the sound of the sea wash over me instead, and feel the air – sharp as a blade this early morning. I get dressed – jeans, jumper, even though it's summer – and run down the stairs and out of the door so I don't have to see either of them or hear any more angry words.

I don't care where I go – I just need to get away fast. A bike would be good but there isn't one so I start running. The sheep sheltering next to the fence scatter, baaing at me as I rush past. 'Stupid things!' I shout, and the wind whips my words away like the gulls, blown and buffeted as if they're just scraps of white paper.

I'm already in the village – village is a huge over-statement – before I even think where I'm going. I'm suddenly self-conscious. People outside the shop are staring at me. I slow down. I guess they don't see that many strangers. They nod when I get nearer, and say *Good Morning* in that soft accent they have here. I keep my head down, don't say anything. Soon as I'm past the shop and the telephone kiosk I start running again.

The road goes over a cattle grid and up a hill. I keep running until my ribs ache. At the top I stop to catch my breath. You can see for miles. The road ribbons its way over the rough moorland; a narrow track forks off and winds all the way back down to the sea and along towards a large white house set on a higher bit of ground. That must be the Manse; Mum pointed it out when the ferry came in, all lit up even at that late hour.

I can see someone fishing off the rocks. I suddenly wish I'd brought a book or something to do, and then I remember the notebook shoved in my pocket so that's OK. I can just go and sit by the sea somewhere and write and I won't look too weird. Then I can work out what to do next. There's no way I'm going back yet.

My phone buzzes in my pocket. Up here you *can* get a signal, then. For a second I let myself hope it's from Sam.

It's a message from Bonnie.

U OK? Have fun! Hope sun shining. xx

I send one back. **Windy! No sun yet**. I pause. I can't tell Bonnie that Mum and Dad are arguing already. I think what to say instead. **Do you remember twin boys at the Manse?**

Bonnie's working this summer on some organic farm in northern Spain. Hannah has a proper job in London. I thought I'd got used to my sisters being away, but it's been much harder this year. Sometimes I make myself think what to do if things get really bad. Like if Mum and Dad actually split up. There's no way I am going to choose which one to live with. I might go and live with Hannah in her flat in London, if she'll have me. Bonnie and I are closer really, but Bonnie lives in a messy student house and there's no spare room.

Another text from Bonnie. **Yes! Weird, remembering. Have u met them?**

I start walking towards the Manse. Might as well go that way as any other. I try sending a reply to Bonnie, but there's no signal. I guess I'm not high enough now. I feel like a tiny ant, a dot on the landscape. No trees. Nowhere to hide. Anyone looking could see me arriving for miles. The figure fishing off the rocks has disappeared.

Closer up, the Manse looks a bit tatty and dilapidated. It's a big house with a walled garden, but the plaster's peeling off the walls. There's no sign of anyone there. But it's early enough for people to be in bed still on a Sunday morning. Or at church. Maybe they all go to church. Everyone's very religious on the

26

island, Mum says. You can't work on a Sunday: you're not even supposed to hang out the washing.

The sound of a car makes me stop. It's an old black taxicab, slowly bumping down the track. I stand back to let it pass, and the driver slows right down, winds down the window and does that old-fashioned thing of lifting his hat, being ever so polite. An old bloke, about fifty, with grey hair and a tweed hat and a weather-beaten face.

'Much obliged,' he says. 'Can we offer you a lift somewhere?'

'No thanks,' I say.

'Enjoying the views?'

'Yes.'

The woman in the passenger seat leans over and smiles. 'You're here for the holidays?'

I nod.

'We'll see you again, then.'

They drive on, bouncing and juddering over the rough ground. I watch them go. The car – taxi – turns into the space by the edge of the Manse and the man and the woman get out and go into the house. The woman's small, grey-haired, wearing a green woolly jumper and a purple skirt. They don't look smart or rich or anything like what I expected from what Mum said.

The boy with the fishing rod walks across the grass and goes into the house too. I'm pretty sure it's the same boy I saw before. Thin dark hair, blue jumper.

What now? I'm cold and starting to get hungry. But it's too soon to walk back. I walk on, past the Manse, and along next to the sea, and on, and on, even though my feet are tired and I don't know where I'm heading any more.

I find a sheltered place to sit, out of the wind and hidden from view. I write in my notebook for a while. When I next look up, the ferry's crossing the Sound, coming slowly towards the island. I watch it come closer, turn and manoeuvre to get into position for docking at the tiny island pier.

I'm so caught up with it that I don't hear the sound of bike wheels until they're right up close and the boy has got off and is coming towards me, smiling. One of the bike wheels spins slowly where he left it on the edge of the track.

'Hey!' he says. 'You again!'

He climbs on the rock next to mine. 'The ferry's nearly in,' he says. 'My brother will be arriving.' He looks at me. 'You're staying in the village: Fiona's house.'

It's a statement; I don't need to answer luckily. For some reason I'm suddenly feeling shy. I notice his eyes: clear, grey-blue. I twist my messy, wind-blown hair back from my face.

'I'm Finn,' he says. 'From the Manse.'

'My sisters knew your brothers,' I say, and immediately wish I hadn't.

He looks at me more closely.

'Way back, when they were seven and nine,' I add. 'I was just a baby.'

'Ah. Ages ago, then,' Finn says. He sounds English; only the very slightest hint of something else. 'You look cold. What are you doing? You've been there for ages.'

I look at him sharply. What business is it of his? I don't like the thought of being watched. I'd thought I was hidden, leant against the rock.

'Why do I have to be doing anything?' I say. It comes out wrong, makes me sound crosser than I am.

'You don't,' Finn says. 'Sorry. Anyway, I've got to go down to the pier now or I'll miss them. Nice to meet you.'

'You too.' I'm embarrassed now about sounding rude. But I can't think what else to say.

He's still hovering there, as if he's waiting for something.

'I'm Kate,' I say, to break the silence.

'Nice name,' he says. He picks up the bike, gets on, pedals off.

I get up, pick up my bag. Meeting him has unsettled me, somehow. I'm too restless to stay sitting there by myself. Too cold. If the ferry is in, the café might open up, and I can get a coffee at least. I make my way along the shore: a short cut back to the village which I couldn't see before. Only it's hard work, walking on damp sand into the wind, and it takes almost as long as the road in the end. I think about the boy called Finn: well-spoken, a bit like the man in the cab who I guess is his dad. Private school, loaded. You can tell that from how confident he is. So, they're one big happy family all on holiday together. About as different from me as I can imagine.

*   *   *

29

The café is open. It's like something out of the 1950s. No cappuccino machine or anything, just coffee from a tin and big china teapots and cups and saucers and tablecloths. At least it's warm and out of the wind and the man behind the counter makes me a toasted sandwich with bacon and the whole thing costs less than £2.50 which you'd never get back home. *No, we can't sell you a whisky*, he tells some old bloke off the ferry; *not on a Sunday. You know that.*

I sit at the window. I'm half looking out for Finn and his brother. Three cars go past with older couples in, and then a muddy jeep driven by a bloke about Bonnie's age with a girl in the front passenger seat and I can't see who else. I guess that might be them, but there's no sign of Finn or his bike.

I finish my sandwich. The café fills up with more people who stare and smile. They all seem to know each other; it's really obvious I don't belong. I decide to go back to the house. *Fiona's* house, Finn called it.

It's dead quiet inside.

'Mum?' I call out as I take off my sandy shoes.

No one's home. Mum's left a note on the table.

We're walking to Hynish Bay. Join us when you wake up! We've left you the map. It's easy to find the way. Hope you slept well. xx

I spread out the map, to see where they've gone. It's miles away. Still, they can talk and sort things out without me having to hear it all. It's weird that they didn't have a clue I was already up and out hours ago.

Odd they didn't check. Maybe that's a good sign. Maybe they made up after their argument and were so wrapped up in each other . . .

There's no point just sitting around here all day. I put my jacket back on and pick up the map and a bottle of water. I find my swimming things too, just in case, and shove everything in my bag. I put on proper walking boots this time and pull the door shut behind me.

The air smells of salt. The wind has dropped a bit and now the sun's higher it feels almost warm. Tiny brown birds flit from one clump of heather to the next. It's so flat you can see for miles. Sea in all directions. The bluest sky, thin wisps of high cloud.

Five

'What did we use to do, when we came here when I was little?' I ask Mum. We're lying at the top of the beach, out of the wind.

'The usual summery things,' Mum says. 'Beaches and sandcastles. Fishing with nets for crabs. Picnics. Bonnie and Hannah played with the other children on the beaches – those boys I mentioned, and their friends. We went for walks sometimes: you in the baby carrier on Dad's back. He'd walk for miles with you, watching the seabirds, rare butterflies, that sort of thing; taking photographs. One year we hired bikes. We went on boat trips. Simple things like that. Everyone was happy.'

She blinks back tears. I look away.

'Are you going to swim?' she asks. 'It'll be freezing, mind.'

I shake my head.

Dad's clambering over the rocks at the far end of the beach. We both watch him: a dark shape silhouetted against the blue backdrop of shining sea. The light's dazzling.

'Shall we go and join him?' I say.

'You go,' Mum says. 'I'm going to lie here in the sun for a while longer.'

'Why doesn't he take photographs any more?' I ask.

Mum shrugs. 'There are lots of things he doesn't do now that he used to do.'

'Like what?'

'Singing. Playing music. He was writing songs and poems when I first met him.'

I look at him. Dad? Singing? I can't imagine it. How come I never knew about that before?

'But he packed a camera to bring with him this holiday,' Mum says wistfully. 'So perhaps he's planning to start taking photos again.'

I find Dad hunkered down next to a huge rock pool. 'Come quietly and have a look at this,' he says. 'Keep your shadow off the water.'

It's a whole other world in there, with its miniature forests and grasses and tiny speckled fish; limpets and anemones and shrimpy things darting across the bottom. Beyond the rocks, the sea rushes and breaks, all sparkly and wild and moving, but the surface of the water in the rock pool is barely ruffled. We both look up as a flock of geese fly over, their wings beating the air in a steady rhythm.

'There's a sight,' Dad says. 'Should've brought the binoculars with us on the walk.'

'Or your camera,' I say pointedly, but he doesn't pick up on it.

'Wild geese. Heading home.' Dad watches them,

and I watch him. He starts saying lines from a poem. Something about being lonely, and the world calling to you, like the geese.

'Mary Oliver,' he says. 'Know it?'

I shake my head.

Dad's already moving on, stepping over the rocks, peering into other pools.

Is Dad lonely? I'm thinking. *Is that what's wrong with him?*

I follow him. 'What's that called?' I point at different coloured seaweeds; tiny fish; red blobs of sea anemone. It's a way to get closer to him: paying attention to the things he likes. It's what Mum should be doing, I think crossly. It's as if she's stopped trying.

'You can eat some of these seaweeds,' Dad says. He shows me something that looks a bit like limp wet lettuce. 'The whole island is a wonderful example of how an ecosystem works.' He explains to me about the machair: the beach-meadows where hundreds of flowers and tiny plants grow on the calcium-rich mix of sand and peat. 'It's one of Europe's rarest ecosystems,' Dad says. 'Created during the Ice Age, from the shells of marine animals that died when sea temperatures dropped. Now, the cattle graze the machair and fertilise it. It's pretty unique, this place.'

Dad points out different birds. He actually sounds cheerful.

'You don't ever talk like this at home,' I say.

Dad hunches his shoulders. 'You don't get a lot of curlews and dunlin and ringed plovers in our bit of the suburbs,' he says. 'Not much seaweed either. And no machair at all.'

'Why do we stay living there, if you hate it so much?' I ask.

'Our jobs. Your school. Friends. My aged parents. The small practicalities of real life and earning a living.' He looks at me. 'I didn't say I hated it, Kate.'

'Not in so many words.'

He doesn't answer that.

'Did you see anything interesting?' Mum asks when I get back to the top of the beach. She's spread out a picnic. 'Want some tea?' She pours out a cup for me from the flask.

'You should have come and looked too,' I tell her.

'I can see well enough from here,' Mum says. 'I've been enjoying the sun. It's more relaxing, up here out of the wind.'

'Did you see the geese?'

'Yes. The wings make a lovely sound, don't they? Your grandma loved to see wild geese.' She passes me a sandwich. I peel it open, pick out the cheese and bits of tomato and leave the bread. Mum frowns but she doesn't say anything.

Dad's slowly making his way back up the beach. He stops every so often to look at things left by the tide. He brings us each a shell. Mine is small and grey-blue, with shiny mother-of-pearl inside. I put it in my jacket pocket. While they eat their lunch, I doodle patterns in the sand with the rib of a feather. The sound of the waves is a constant background roar, smoothing out

35

my mind and washing it clean. I feel a long way from home, from anyone really. Today, I don't mind. It's strangely restful, stopping thinking for a change.

The three of us doze in the sun: even Dad. Mum's turned away, on her side. When I next look round, I notice Dad's hand on the small of her back, just resting there. I close my eyes again. Maybe it is going to be all right, after all.

The walk home is peaceful too, to begin with: we don't talk much. We're all gradually getting used to a different pace: *island time*, Mum calls it. Every so often a car or tractor rumbles along the road and we have to stand up on the bank at the edge of the single-track road to let it pass, but there's hardly any traffic really.

The sound of an engine roaring up behind us makes us stop still and stand well back. 'Idiots!' Dad shouts. 'Slow down!'

It's the mud-splattered jeep from the ferry. It brakes suddenly, slows right down and stops. For a second I think Dad's going to start having a go at the driver, but before he can say anything, someone's calling my name. 'Hey, Kate!'

It's Finn. He's in the front passenger seat, leaning out to wave at me. I'm so surprised I wave back. I guess the driver is one of his older brothers: he looks a bit similar, but with longer, crazier hair. He grins. 'Want a lift? Not much space, but we don't mind if you don't!'

Dad and Mum both look confused.

'No thanks,' I say quickly. 'We want to walk.'

'OK.' The jeep pulls forwards again. I hear someone say something: a girl's voice. Finn turns and looks out of the window, back at me. I feel myself blush.

'I met him earlier,' I say. 'He's the boy we saw running near the house, Mum.'

'They ought to know better,' Dad says. 'Driving like that on this road.'

'I expect they know the road pretty well,' Mum says. 'They're the lads from the Manse. The girls used to play with the twins, remember? They'll have been along here hundreds of times.'

Dad grumbles under his breath. 'No excuse for dangerous driving. Fools. They'll come off the road if they're not careful.'

Why does Dad have to spoil everything? It's a reference to Sam's driving, obviously. For my benefit.

Mum tries to smooth things over. She talks about the time when Bonnie and Hannah joined in a sand-castle competition with the boys from the Manse. They made a sand volcano: one of the boys made an actual fire in the top, so it would smoke like a real volcano. But they still didn't win . . . Dad says he doesn't remember. He points out a field where you can see corncrakes, according to the guidebook back at the house.

I walk behind them. I can't stop thinking about Sam now I've started. What's he doing, right now? Is he thinking about me? What's going to happen to him? Does he blame me?

It seems a long way back to the house. My feet ache.

I make myself think about Bonnie instead, on her Spanish farm. I imagine her in bright sunshine, the golden light as afternoon merges into evening. I wish I was there with her. Anywhere but here.

Six

Tuesday morning. Dad's gone out with the binoculars to watch birds on the loch; Mum's having coffee with Fiona, who owns our house and lives on the mainland usually but is staying at the hotel this week. I didn't even know there was a hotel.

So, it's just me, looking for something to do.

I've even been to the one-room museum (ten minutes max to see everything), and now I'm busy reading the noticeboard outside the village shop (Ceilidh on Friday night: all welcome; wetsuits for sale; sheepdog puppies ready end of August; meeting about the wind farm project).

I hear voices. Finn, and the older boy who was driving, and a girl about the same age with long straight dark hair, are coming out of the shop loaded up with plastic carrier bags.

'Finn, it's your friend again!' the boy says.

This time it's Finn who blushes. But he quickly recovers himself. 'Kate,' he introduces me. 'My brother Piers and this is his friend Thea.'

He emphasises the word *friend* and everyone laughs.

'Hello,' I say.

Thea smiles and holds out her hand to shake mine. This is a bit weird, of course – old-fashionedly polite, like the dad – but I don't mind really so I shake her hand and then Piers's too. (I have to ask Dad how to spell the name – Peers? Pierce? It's Middle or Old English, apparently. There's a medieval poem called *Piers Plowman*.)

'We're going to have a barbecue on the beach later,' Piers says. 'You should come. Shouldn't she, Finn?' He turns to me again. 'Finn could do with some company of his own age.'

'Piers, stop it!' Thea says. 'Ignore him, Kate.'

'I don't mind,' I say. 'Thanks. It sounds good.'

'You can come back to the Manse with us now. We'll wait in the jeep, up by the telephone box, while you tell your parents.'

'Sorry. He's so bossy,' Thea says. 'He's used to being in charge.'

'Someone has to be!' Piers says.

I quite like it. It means I don't have to decide what to do: they all just assume I'll come along, and seeing as I don't have any plans of my own I might as well.

'I'll write a note for Mum,' I say. 'I won't be long.'

Finn walks to the house with me and waits at the gate while I go inside and write the note and grab my bag and a coat. I check my hair in the mirror quickly – not that it matters very much, seeing as the wind will mess it up the minute I go outside.

I go to the front door and call to Finn. 'Should I bring anything with me?'

He shakes his head. 'No, we got everything we need at the shop.'

The jeep rattles and bumps and jolts and it's impossible to stay sitting upright. I keep falling against Finn, next to me in the back with all the bags of shopping. He laughs. Piers puts a disc into the jeep's CD player and suddenly music is blasting out: piano and violins and saxophone: quite beautiful and haunting and a bit weird, like nothing I've ever heard before.

'I'll turn your symphony down a bit,' Thea says. 'We don't want to upset your parents.'

'Joy and Alex won't mind!' Piers shouts back. 'They *like* my stuff, actually!'

'Not at this volume!' Thea turns round in the front seat to talk to me. 'Piers's and Finn's parents are amazing,' she says. 'You'll love them. Everybody does. They are incredibly kind and generous. There are going to be at least ten people staying at the Manse this summer.'

'Not all at the same time,' Finn says. 'And there's only us at the moment. Jamie's coming down with Tim and the London crew at the weekend.'

For a moment I'm imagining a whole *film* crew – till I realise it's just what posh people call a group of friends.

Thea explains. 'Jamie is Piers's twin. Finn's other brother. Tim's an old friend of Jamie and Piers, but

41

he's sort of everyone's friend now. He's been coming here for years, every summer. He loves the island almost as much as Finn does. And Joy and Alex love him like another son.'

'I think I saw your parents before,' I tell Finn. 'Driving an old taxicab.'

'That's them!' Thea says. 'Crazy, yes? To still be driving that old thing on these roads with all the potholes. But they like old things. They keep everything until it falls apart. Literally!'

We've arrived at the Manse. Piers parks the jeep in the layby near the house and we pile out with all the shopping and walk round to the back door, which is already open.

The kitchen's large, old-fashioned, with a range and a big wooden table and chairs, everything a bit tatty. We stack the bags on the table and Thea starts putting things in cupboards. Piers fills the kettle and puts it on the range. Finn gets out mugs for tea.

'We can't get a fire going for the barbecue till the tide's gone down,' Finn explains. 'We've got our own bit of beach but only at low tide.' He looks at his watch. 'In about two hours.'

Two whole hours! I'm going to be here all day at that rate. I'm suddenly shy, tongue-tied.

But I needn't have worried. Everyone else talks practically non-stop. They talk about music, and books, and their friend Tim, who has a new job as some sort of sales rep for a publisher and so gets a company car. I work out that they are all students, apart from Finn (still at school, one year to go) and

Tim. Piers is studying for a PhD in music and wants to be a composer. His twin, Jamie, plays lead guitar in a band. Their parents are retired now, but Joy was a scientist and Alex worked as an antiquarian bookseller, which explains why the Manse is full to bursting with books, old prints and paintings. It even *smells* of old things: musty, slightly damp.

They start discussing some of the jobs that need to be done now everyone's here for the holidays.

'We need to get the peat in,' Joy says. 'We're already late. Most of the crofters did theirs way back in June. We've cut most of it, but it's got to be brought back here and stacked so it will dry and be ready for winter. If everyone helps it won't be so exhausting.'

'Of course.' Thea nods.

Joy seems to notice me for the first time. 'You're the girl we passed on the road the other day, aren't you?' she says. 'You've all met already, then.'

'Poor Kate didn't stand a chance,' Thea says. 'We whisked her up and brought her here for the barbecue.'

'You're not an island girl though?'

'No. Just on holiday,' I say. 'I hope it's all right, me being here.'

Joy smiles. 'Of course it's all right. You are very welcome. It will be nice for Finn.'

Everyone keeps saying that. Why? I wonder.

Joy seems old for a mum. But then, she has grown-up children as well as Finn. But Mum does too, and Joy seems much older than Mum. Not just the grey hair and the glasses. Her clothes, perhaps. And her hands, and the way she speaks.

Alex comes downstairs. He watches everyone from the kitchen doorway. His eyes twinkle at me, as if he's pleased I'm there too, but he doesn't say much. Finn pours tea for everyone from a big brown pot. A marmalade cat sidles in and winds in and out of everyone's legs under the table before jumping up and settling itself on Joy's lap. Piers wanders off and a few minutes later the house is full of the sound of piano music: loud chords and impossibly intricate notes.

'What are you going to cook on the barbecue?' Joy asks.

'Sausages, veggy kebabs, mackerel if Finn can catch some!' Thea says.

Finn looks at me. 'Want to come and catch fish?'

I've never been fishing before so I just watch. It's cold, mind. I wrap myself up in the old blanket we brought from the house to sit on. You're not supposed to make a noise when you fish, apparently, so we don't talk. Every so often I forget, and ask Finn a question, and he answers very quietly. He's too polite to tell me to shut up.

'Do Alex and Joy live here all year round?' I ask.

'Only since last year, when they both retired. They bought the Manse for our holidays originally, way back when houses were cheap as chips.'

'So do you come here every holiday?'

'Yes.'

'Don't you get bored? Wouldn't you like to see other places?'

Finn stares at me as if I'm crazy. 'No. I'm never

bored. I'd live here all the time if I had my way. I can't wait to leave school and then I can.'

'Where's your school?'

'London.'

'That's a very long way away!'

He takes a coloured spinner from the open box by his side and fixes it to the line.

'I go to an ordinary comprehensive school,' I tell him, even though he hasn't asked. 'What's it like, boarding?'

'Rubbish. A total nightmare, if you really want to know.'

I stop asking questions for a while.

I study his face in profile: serious, thin, fine-boned. His eyes are grey-blue and his hair dark, curling at the back along his neck. Pale skin. He seems perfectly at home, perched on the rocks, almost camouflaged in his big baggy jumper: hand-knitted flecked blue wool. He casts the line, and skilfully makes the spinner dance and zigzag like a tiny fish darting through the water.

'We should have come down earlier,' he says. 'It's best at high tide, catching mackerel off the rocks. This state of an ebb tide you need a boat really. We could go and get the boat I suppose . . .'

I remember what Mum said about the house parties and boats. *It looked fun*, she said.

'I'll take you out in it sometime, if you like,' he says. 'It's just a wooden rowing boat, nothing grand.'

'Is it dangerous,' I say, 'with all the rocks and the currents and tides and all that?'

'Not if you know what you are doing,' Finn says. 'I've been coming here since I was a small child. We could go to one of the uninhabited islands, to get cockles. We do that every summer.'

I'm not exactly sure what cockles are. Shellfish, I guess, like in that old song: '*cockles and mussels, alive, alive-o*'. But I'm not going to show myself up by asking.

Finn suddenly springs into action – leaping up, winding in the line on the rod, flicking a thrashing, shiny fish on the stone. He unhooks it and hits it on the rock to kill it. It lies there, silver with beautiful markings along its back. He does this six times, until he has six gleaming mackerel of the right size to barbecue. Each time, it makes my eyes smart to watch the fish die. 'The fish hardly suffer,' Finn says when he sees me flinch. 'They have a good life. It's better than factory farming.'

I hear voices. Piers and Thea are making their way down towards us with baskets and bags of stuff. Thea waves. 'Caught anything?' she calls.

'Six fish!' I call back.

'Excellent.' Thea clambers down over the rocks and puts everything down while she takes off her shoes. She walks along the damp sand, her bare feet sinking in and leaving perfect footprints. I notice how pale and narrow her feet are: fine, thin toes with pale pink nails. 'Come and help make the fire,' she says to me. 'We need driftwood; want to go and see if you can find some dry stuff?'

I take my own shoes off and walk along the top of the beach, picking up bits of wood. There isn't much that's dry. The wind's blowing in off the sea. Small brown and white birds scurry along at the edge of the water, so fast they look funny: as if they are scooting along on roller skates. The waves roll in, lines of white breakers curling over and spreading on to the pale sand in loops of lace.

By the time I've walked along the whole length of sand and back, Piers and Thea have made a fireplace out of stones and have started the fire.

'Thanks, Kate,' Thea says as I dump my armful of wood. She feeds small sticks into the flames, adds bigger bits. I pull my collar up higher and hug my knees for warmth.

Piers and Finn thread chunks of onion and red pepper and mushrooms on to sticks. 'It will be ages before the fire's hot enough for cooking,' Finn tells me. 'Hope you're not in a rush.'

'No,' I say. 'I've got all day. And all evening. All week, in fact!'

He laughs. 'Good.'

Piers hums a tune as he gets everything ready. I'm a bit in awe of him. He seems grown-up, older than Bonnie or Holly but he can't be really. He reminds me of someone – that Hugh person on telly, I decide, who cooks outside like this, on a beach, with freshly caught fish and seaweed or whatever. He starts talking to Thea about friends, and films, and some book they've been reading about science and religion.

'Are you too cold?' Finn asks me after a while.

I am, but I don't want to say I am. None of them

seems the least bit bothered by the cold. I suppose they are used to it.

'Want to run along the beach and back with me?'

'OK.'

I go slowly to begin with, but it's fun; a bit like being a child again. The wind whips my hair and the waves make such a racket as they crash on to the sand I can hardly hear what Finn's saying.

I'm out of breath way before he is. 'You go on,' I say, and he does, in that loping stride he was doing the first time I saw him, pebbles spilling out of his pockets.

But he doesn't just run on; he loops back to rejoin me, and we go on side by side together. 'Seen the ringing stone yet?' he asks me.

'No. What is it?'

'A lump of granite, from the Ice Age probably, brought here from a different island. Millions of years old. It's covered in cup marks made by Bronze Age people. Some sort of pre-Druid religious rite, people think. To do with fertility, or blood sacrifice, or star charts or stone worship. No one has a clue really.'

'I think there was something about it in that tiny museum,' I say. 'Where is it, exactly?'

'Over on the east coast. You go along the machair for another two miles or so and then cross over to the other side of the island. There's something extraordinary about it: one of those special places, you know? Where time seems to collapse: the past and the present come together.'

I look sceptically back at him. 'Yes?'

He laughs. 'Honestly! The look on your face! Anyway, it's too far to go there now. We'll go another time. Run back? I'll race you.'

'Absolutely not,' I say. But I start running, to get a few seconds' head start.

'Hey!' he shouts, and catches up. 'That's cheating!'

'It was my only chance.' I laugh. 'And I'm not sorry!'

He matches his pace to mine and we run along the firm sand nearer the water.

I'm puffed out and hot by the time we're only half-way back. We walk the rest of the way. He keeps stopping to look at things: a shell, an interesting pebble, a piece of unusual seaweed, a crab shell, the V-shaped marks made by a bird's feet. I think, briefly, of Dad. Finn, like a younger version of Dad, or what Dad might have been like when he was sixteen, seventeen.

'Stop there!' Finn says. 'Shut your eyes and hold out your hand.'

I do as he says. I feel something cool, damp in my palm. For a brief second, Finn's warm hand closes around my cold one.

'Now look.'

It's just a pebble. A pretty pebble, still wet and shiny from the sea.

'Thank you,' I say. I slip it into my pocket for safe keeping.

Joy and Alex come down to the beach just as the fire is at the white-hot charcoal stage and the sausages are almost cooked: Finn's laying the gutted fish side by side on the grill over the fire. The meat and fish spit hot fat into the fire and it smells amazing. Alex is carrying two camping chairs and a bottle of whisky; Joy's brought rugs and glasses and plates. They've obviously done this a hundred times before; it's nothing special to them, but for me it's all new.

Joy wraps me in a big tartan rug. Alex offers me a glass of whisky. 'For medicinal purposes. Your lips are blue with the cold.'

I take one sip to try it. It's totally disgusting. I hand the glass back, spluttering. 'No thanks! Too strong.'

'Food always tastes better outside,' Joy says, laughing and settling back into her chair with her plate on her lap.

'You always say that!' Piers opens another bottle of beer and passes one to Thea.

'And it's always true.' Joy smiles. 'Tuck in, everyone.'

Alex surveys the beach with binoculars. 'Sanderlings,' he says, 'and a curlew sandpiper.' He passes the binoculars to Finn.

I eat my food. Joy's right: everything does taste delicious. I'm the happiest I have been for ages, wrapped in a tartan rug on a rock at the top of a huge sandy beach, watching the waves roll in. I join in the conversation when I can think of something sensible to say, but mostly I'm just quiet, taking it all in. No one bothers me, or pesters me with stupid questions, or makes a fuss.

* * *

'We'll give you a lift back, Kate,' Piers says, when we're packing everything up to take back to the house. 'Just say when you want to go.'

'Thanks,' I say. 'Do you know what time it is?'

Alex pulls an old-fashioned watch out of his jacket pocket. 'Ten minutes to seven.'

I've been here for hours. I'd no idea. 'I'd better go back straight away,' I say. 'But I don't mind walking, honestly.'

'Don't be ridiculous,' Piers says. 'Of course I'll drive you back. We'll dump the stuff at home and then I'm all yours.'

Everyone walks back together to the Manse. Joy chats to me as we climb up over the grassy bank to the house. 'You must come round whenever you want to,' she says. 'We keep an open house. The more the merrier, as far as I'm concerned.'

'Absolutely,' Piers says.

'It must be a bit lonely by yourself, with both your sisters away,' Joy says. She thinks she possibly remembers them, but it was a long time ago, and there have been so many friends, over the years: people on their holidays, children on the beach . . .

I don't want to leave without thanking Finn, but the kitchen's full of people and Piers is grabbing the keys for the jeep and when I look round to say goodbye, he's disappeared.

Thea grabs her coat. 'I'll come for the ride too.' She goes to the kitchen door and calls up the stairs. 'Finn? You coming to take Kate home?' But he doesn't answer, and Piers is already walking out of the back door.

I scurry after him.

Piers drives fast. But you can see for miles that there's nothing coming: just a few cows and sheep grazing on the grass either side of the single-track road, and he knows every pothole and bump by heart. We rattle over the cattle grid at the beginning of the village. Piers pulls over at a passing place to let a van go by, and then we're passing the shop and the museum and we're back at the house. He stops on the grass by the gate. 'There you go. See you soon.'

Thea leans over and kisses my cheek. 'Yes, come again soon, Kate. It's much more fun with lots of people.'

'Thanks for everything,' I say. 'Say thanks to Finn for me too.'

'I will.' She smiles. 'I don't know why he didn't say goodbye.'

'Because he's Finn,' Piers says.

I watch them drive off. Piers toots the horn and a flock of little brown speckled birds take off from the grass all together, twittering madly.

I take a deep breath and go inside.

Seven

'Where have you been all this time?' Mum says, the moment I set foot in the door. 'We've been worried sick.'

'I left you a note.'

'This morning, yes! It is now nearly half past seven in the evening, Kate!'

'Sorry,' I say. Though I don't see why I should be. 'I didn't think you'd mind me having a nice time.'

'What does that mean?' Mum looks furious.

'Nothing,' I say innocently. 'But you and Dad are doing your own thing . . . I thought you'd be pleased I was too.'

She calms down a bit, recovers herself. 'Yes, well, of course I'm pleased you're meeting people and having fun. I was worried, that's all.'

'Well, don't be. There's no need to worry. Not about me, anyway.' I go upstairs before she can say anything back, and get my things ready for a shower. Only there's no hot water.

I lie on my bed instead, and listen to the sound of the

sea through the open skylight. I let my mind go over the day; gather all the fragments together and relive each moment. The messy, comfortable kitchen. Fishing with Finn. Making the fire. Running along the beach with Finn. Finn cooking the silver mackerel. The sweet smell of woodsmoke and charred fish. Everyone talking and laughing and drinking and eating together. The rhythmic sound of waves rolling on to the shore.

I put my hand in my jeans' pocket and look more closely at the pebble that Finn gave me. It was wet and shiny before; now it has dried and faded, but it's still pretty: charcoal grey speckled with silvery sparkly bits. He made me close my eyes, and open my hand. He closed my fingers over the damp pebble, and for a second he held his hand over mine. It felt warm, and comforting.

Sam's face swims into my mind . . . I open my eyes abruptly.

Dad's calling up the stairs. 'Kate? We thought we'd go out to the hotel for dinner tonight. Can you be ready in half an hour or so?'

I go to the top of the stairs. 'I've already eaten,' I tell him. 'I'm not hungry.'

Dad frowns. 'You sure? What did you have?'

'Barbecue food,' I say. 'Fish and sausages and vegetable kebabs. Masses of it. I'm totally full up.'

'OK,' he says slowly. 'Well, do you mind if we go out without you, then?'

''Course not,' I say. I don't say I'm glad. In my heart I'm willing them to try harder, to be fun and nice to each other. Like they used to be.

I imagine Finn's family at the Manse, playing games and listening to Piers on the piano and talking intelligently about books and films and music.

I listen to Mum getting herself ready to go out. That's a good sign. She's putting make-up on in the bathroom, chatting away. It will be so much better, just the two of them eating dinner together. Maybe Mum will have wine, and relax, get giggly, lighten up a bit.

When they've gone, I switch the boost on the water heater, so I can have a long, hot bath. I leave a trail of fine silver sand behind me all the way down the stairs, and a bigger heap when I strip off my jeans in the bathroom.

After my bath, I flick through the pile of leaflets about the island on the living room table. Finn would know all this sort of stuff. It says about Viking raids, and Norse settlers. Gaelic names, and Viking ones. There's another leaflet about birds.

I sit in the window seat, with its view of the sea, all the way out to the islands. They look further away this evening: grey, low on the horizon under a grey sky. The sea looks grey too, with white flecks on the waves. The tide's coming back in; the waves break in long smooth lines along the beach, spreading out over the sand in shallow white froth. A break in the cloud lets a ray of sunlight through, catching the water and turning it silver.

It's late when I hear Mum and Dad come back in. They talk in soft voices; I can't hear what they're saying but

Mum laughs. Good. Doors open and close. It goes quiet again. I relax back into sleep.

Much later, I wake in the pitch dark to the sound of the wind battering the house so hard that everything's shaking. The sea is roaring. Rain spatters against the skylights. The storm lasts all night: every time I wake, the wind seems louder, howling and crying as if it's a wild animal that wants to be let in.

Eight

By morning the rain has stopped and the sky is clearing. I get out of bed and go downstairs: no one else is up. There's no sound from Mum and Dad's room. That's hopeful, I guess. I make tea and toast, then put on my boots and step outside. I set off up the road away from the village, no real plan. The air smells clean, rain-washed.

I'm zinging with energy. It's as if the night storm has cleared something in me too. I've suddenly come to life again: my senses awake in a different way. I know this sounds weird, but it's as if the colour has come back in: brighter, sharper. I'm seeing everything more vividly as I walk along, like a film, except that I am in the film and I can hear and smell as well as see it all. A dazzling patch of sunlight on sea; a flock of geese grazing along the grass next to a shining stretch of puddle on the field; small brown birds flitting from one fence post to another. The geese start honking and all take off in flight, necks outstretched, wings slowly beating together.

The island is almost flat just here, and there's this huge overarching sky, clouds moving fast, light changing every second, bringing different things into focus, like a spotlight. A white house; the sweep of pale sand; the grassy dunes, a line of telegraph poles; the gleaming ribbon of wet road.

A small red fishing boat is making its way out of the old harbour, pitching and dropping as it ploughs through the waves. I think about what Finn said, about going out in his boat to get cockles. Will he remember?

I stop at a fork in the road. Which way?

A brown hare races across the field to the left: I go that way. The road curves round, over a small hill and then back down the other side, to a part of the island I haven't seen before. There are houses scattered along the road, none of them close together. Everywhere you look, in fact, there are small white houses, tucked in corners of fields, or against a bank. Crofters, I suppose. I try to remember what Alex was saying about them yesterday, on the beach. Something about the land being divided up into crofts and each one having a mixture of different kinds of ground: fertile bits and less fertile, and an area of peat bank, all shared out fairly. I should have listened more carefully.

I try to imagine what it might be like, to love a particular place as much as Finn seems to. I've always lived in the suburbs, in a sort of non-place: mostly housing estates, long straight roads hemmed in by brick and concrete and glass buildings. Shops, garages, warehouses, takeaway places, cafés, pubs. Roads full of traffic – that roaring sound always in the background, of cars, and sirens; planes overhead – the sky scored by vapour trails. There's the park near Sam's nan's house, where we used to go sometimes, our special tree . . .

What will Sam be doing today? He hasn't phoned or texted once. I don't even know where he's living, now his nan won't let him stay at her place overnight . . .

Is he angry?

Is he missing me?

Does he think about me *at all*?

They'll be waking up in the Manse. Coming down for breakfast together in the cosy kitchen. Perhaps Piers and Thea are still sleeping . . . are they girlfriend and boyfriend? I couldn't tell yesterday. They seemed close, but I didn't see them touch or hold hands or kiss. Maybe posh people don't do that in public. Maybe it's not polite.

It begins to drizzle. I pull up the hood on my jacket. No one's going to see so it doesn't matter what I look like. The road narrows; there's another cattle grid to cross, and a cluster of houses sheltering behind a thick hedge. The view opens up again suddenly: a ruined house, a broad stretch of flowering meadow above a wide sandy beach. The sea is turquoise-blue even in the rain. Fingers of rock dissect the white sweep of shell sand. Beyond, other islands: layers upon layers of islands, a whole archipelago.

I shelter in the ruined house for a while to see if the rain stops. But it doesn't, and so I go on in the rain, along the grassy path to the left, round the top of the beach, past a herd of black shaggy-haired cows and calves, along and on and on next to the sea. All the way, I find smaller beaches, sheltered sandy coves. I must have walked miles, and I've seen no one.

The rain stops and I clamber down over rocks on to a small beach and sit there, watching the sea and the changing light, until even the birds stop noticing me. Little scurrying brown ones like I saw before, and black and white ones with red legs, and smaller ones that swoop and weave through the air like sea swallows.

I pull my phone out of my pocket. No signal. I realise I haven't checked my phone for over twenty-four hours.

'A boy called,' Dad tells me when I get back. He's sitting outside the house at the wooden picnic table, reading the newspaper.

'Was it Finn?' I ask.

'He didn't say his name. Dark-haired, about your age.'

'And? What did he say?'

'I think he was going to invite you to something, but as you weren't here, he didn't.'

'What was it? The something.'

'He didn't say. At least, I don't think he did.'

'Dad! How can you be so annoying! How long ago was he here?'

'An hour ago? Where did you go so early, anyway?'

'I went for a walk.'

Dad smiles. 'Yes, but where to?'

'I don't know! I don't know the names of everywhere, do I? Just a walk across the island. Right to the other side.'

I go inside to find Mum. She doesn't know any more than Dad does. She makes me eat more breakfast, which I do, seeing as I only had toast and I've been walking for hours and I'm suddenly starving.

'Would you like us to hire you a bike?' Mum says. 'Then you could get around more easily by yourself. It would only take about ten minutes to cycle to the Manse from here, and you could find out what Finn wanted.'

But I've used up all my energy. And I don't want to look so pathetically desperate, chasing after Finn. I lie on my bed and read one of the magazines from the pile under the telly table.

I keep wondering what I'm missing. The boat trip? Another barbecue? The peat-cutting expedition? Now I wish I hadn't got up so early and gone out for so long.

'Kate?' Mum calls upstairs. 'We thought we'd get bikes for all three of us. After lunch. It'll be fun. We can explore a bit further afield.'

'No thanks,' I call back. 'You and Dad should, though.'

Because maybe he'll come back. Perhaps they'll be driving somewhere, and will drop in here first, on the off-chance. I can't help myself hoping.

But no one calls. The day drifts away. I watch the bit of beach you can see from the front window. A fishing boat goes out, stacked high with red and orange buoys, and men in yellow waterproofs balancing as the boat bucks and tips. It begins to rain again. The sky is grey, except far out to sea there's a strip of bright silver where sunlight must be shining through. Next time I look, it's gone.

Dad comes back first, freewheeling down the last bit of road before the village. He gets off and wheels the bike over the grass to the gate. He waves at me at the window as he goes past and I wave back. He's dripping wet. He stamps his feet in the porch and swears under his breath.

'What happened to Mum?' I ask him.

'Stopped to shelter. Put the kettle on, Kate.'

He tells me about the bike ride while I make us tea. Four seals in the bay over the other side from here; they met someone who'd seen basking sharks.

'Why didn't you wait for Mum?'

'You know what she's like. She wanted me to go on; she's so much slower than I am.'

'Honestly, Dad!'

He shrugs.

I still don't understand why he wouldn't want to slow down and go along beside her. It's what most people would do, wouldn't they? Even with someone who was just a friend. It's not as if there's any rush. The whole point is doing something *together*.

When she finally gets back, Mum's in a foul mood.

There was something wrong with the bike. She had to push the last two miles. She's practically in tears.

Dad doesn't say anything.

'Tea, Mum?' I ask. 'Shall I run you a bath?'

She nods. 'Thanks. You made the right choice, staying here. I'm completely soaked. And the bike was rubbish.'

'It was you who said we didn't need to bring the car over,' Dad says.

Mum glares at him. 'I said I didn't want to drive on the island. What's that got to do with anything?'

I leave them to it.

From the bathroom I can hear their voices: Dad's horribly level, rational tone of voice going on at Mum, while she gets more and more upset and angry . . .

The downstairs bedroom door slams.

I can't stand this any longer. I find my jacket, and pull on boots, and go out.

I walk fast. My heart's racing, my stomach twisted with worry. By the time I've been walking for half an hour I've calmed down a bit. The rain's stopped; the wind's dropped too, so the air is filled with different sounds: birds, and the waves, and the hum of bees on the machair. I walk past an old man and a boy herding three shaggy black cows out of a field and down the road, and the man raises his hand to me and says hello. It's like a scene in a film, or a book, or something. It could be happening a hundred years ago. Perhaps it is. I glance back: they're walking slowly, man and boy: the man's holding the last cow's tail in one hand as if he is steering it along. The boy's dressed the same as the man: waterproof jacket, cords, boots. But they are real, and it is now.

I remember what Finn said about that stone. Places where time *collapses*. That would be weird, wouldn't it, if you could be somewhere and just walk into the past like that? Not time travel exactly but to do with the way things go on happening in one place . . . like stepping through a gap in time, or because of some sort of emotional connection . . . when you are feeling something very strongly . . .

I realise there are tears on my face; I'm actually crying as I walk along. What's happening with Mum and Dad . . . watching everything unravel . . . and there's nothing I can do about it . . . I know it happens to lots of people, their parents split, and I've always thought it was the worst possible thing to happen and now it is going to happen to me.

Bonnie says all couples argue; it's perfectly fine and healthy and normal in a relationship. Arguing doesn't mean everything's wrong. But she's hardly ever around these days. She doesn't hear what I hear. I never see them make up after they've argued. Dad's so distant and cold. And Mum doesn't even try to make things fun any more. It's as if she's given up. They seem more and more different from each other. They don't even want to do the same things on holiday.

Luckily no cars pass me and there's no one to see me crying. Eventually I stop.

I have never been anywhere where the sky seemed so huge. Mum says it's because the island is almost flat. Sea in every direction. It's so far out in the ocean the weather changes all the time, and the light changes too, so you see things that were invisible before, like the other islands in the distance. They seem to come and go, as if sometimes they are there, and sometimes not . . .

Nothing stays the same for long.

I hear a car engine, getting closer. I stop to look back. It's a Land Rover or a jeep, I see now, and my heart gives a little leap. I stand back at one of the passing places to let it go by. It clatters over the next cattle grid, and then slows down, and I can see I was right to be hopeful. Piers is driving, and Finn is in the front passenger seat.

'Where are you off to now?' Piers asks. 'Can we give you a lift?'

'Just walking . . . not going anywhere in particular.' It sounds lame.

Piers laughs. 'We called for you this morning,' he said. 'But you were out walking then too. We thought you might come with us on a wee boating trip. To get cockles. Tomorrow or the next day, depending on the weather. When the wind drops, at least.'

'Yes please,' I say.

'Why don't you get in? We're off to get fresh lobster from Isla's dad. Come for the ride.'

'Kate's wanting to walk, Piers!' Finn says.

'No,' I say quickly. "I'd like to come with you. Thanks.'

Piers turns the music up so loud there's no point even trying to talk. It's good, bowling along in the jeep, leaving my sad thoughts behind for a while at least.

We turn off up a narrow track and bump all the way to an old white cottage at the top. There's a sign: *Fresh lobsters for sale*. While Piers goes in, I stay in the jeep with Finn. He switches off the music.

'Sorry,' Finn says. 'Piers is impossible sometimes.'

'What do you mean?'

'The way he just crashes over anyone else's plans. But he means well.'

'I know that,' I say.

'Where were you going really?'

'Just walking. To get out of the house. It's unbearable. My parents . . .'

Finn turns so he's looking at me. 'What's going on?'

'Arguing and stuff. It's always like this now. I think they're going to split up.'

He doesn't say anything.

A girl comes out of the house and stands there a moment. She's really pretty. I glance at Finn, but he hasn't seen her. The girl goes back inside.

Piers comes out carrying a plastic bucket and passes it to me to put on the back seat. The lobsters are still alive, clattering over each other, shiny blue. He puts the lid on and clicks it tight. 'Can you

66

hold the bucket steady so the water doesn't slop everywhere?'

'I'll do that,' Finn says. 'Swap seats?

'Isla was asking after you,' Piers says to Finn. 'I gave her your best wishes. I invited her to come out with us in the boat too.'

'What did she say?'

'She said she'd love to.'

Piers starts up the engine. He turns the jeep in front of the house and skids on loose gravel. I see a face at the window: that girl again, who I imagine must be Isla. For a moment our eyes meet but neither of us smiles or waves or anything.

'You're quiet,' Piers says to me.

'She's fine,' Finn says. 'Don't take any notice, Kate.'

I haven't got anything interesting to say . . . my head's a blank. But Piers doesn't seem that bothered, he chats on to Finn about wetsuits and windsurfing, and I look out of the window. The lobsters clatter and scrabble in their plastic bucket. It's a horrible sound.

'Come back for tea with us,' Finn says, when we're almost back at the village.

'Are you sure?' I say. 'Thanks.'

He's being kind. He knows I don't want to go back to my house.

'Can we stop a minute, so I can tell my parents where I am?'

Piers slows the jeep down as we get to the house, and pulls up on the grass in front.

Dad's reading in the front window seat. He waves through the window.

I run inside.

'I'm having tea at the Manse,' I tell him. 'They're waiting for me in the jeep so I can't stop.' I run out again before he has a chance to say anything.

Nine

The Manse sitting room is cosy with old sofas and soft chairs and a green carpet, and on every surface there are piles of newspapers, letters and bits of paper.

Finn seems distracted. He leafs through a pile of papers on one of the chintzy armchairs. 'You know about the wind farm project?' he says.

I shake my head.

'There's a plan to build a huge wind farm just off the west coast of the island.'

'Isn't that a good thing?' I say.

'No!' Finn huffs. 'It most certainly is not. It's a massive disaster on every count. It will totally ruin this island. And the so-called public consultation's a joke. There's big money involved, of course. There always is. Business interests. Politics. It's totally corrupt.'

I think for a bit about what I can say that doesn't make me look like a total idiot. 'I thought wind energy was a good idea,' I say. 'Like it's green, and renewable, and better than nuclear power stations. Isn't it?'

'Well, yes, but it's the scale of this project, and where they are planning to put it,' Finn says. 'Each turbine will be HUGE, built up on a platform, and they'll be lit up at night. Because the island is so flat you'll be able to see them from all over the island. Five kilometres is ridiculously close. And they're planning maybe five hundred turbines, could be seven hundred. Bigger than any of the existing wind farms. The government want to pour money into it because it's part of some strategy for renewable energy for the UK, but they haven't thought any of it through. For a start the waves round this island are too high: even the maintenance boats won't be able to get through most of the year. And wind power's incredibly inefficient.'

Piers comes in. 'Talking about the wind farm by any chance, Finn? Kate's got that glazed-over look!'

I so have not, I'm about to say . . . but just in time I realise it's only banter between brothers. He's winding Finn up.

Finn scowls. 'You'll be the first to complain when they do build it, Piers.'

'If.' Piers sits down with us at the table and pours himself tea. 'Urgh. Cold!' He leans forwards. 'So, Kate, what's your view?'

'I – I don't really know. I've only just heard about it.'

'Well, you'll hear a lot more. Finn's obsessed. But don't let him brainwash you.'

Finn looks furious. 'Have you finished?' he says to Piers. 'Why don't you go and cook your lobsters or do something useful?'

70

'Good idea.'

Finn's quiet once Piers has left. I don't know what to say. I finish my tea. Perhaps I should just go.

'About the boat trip,' I say. 'Is it still OK for me to come?'

He looks up. 'Yes, of course. We'll go tomorrow if it's fair. Everything depends on the weather here. I expect you've noticed.'

I nod.

'Sorry about your parents,' Finn says. 'You know – the arguing and that. Do you want to talk about it?'

'No,' I say. 'Thanks though.'

I'm embarrassed now. As if my worries are of any interest to Finn. 'I'd better go back,' I say. 'I'll walk. I like the walk.'

'Listen to the shipping forecast,' Finn says. 'Late tonight or early tomorrow morning on the radio. So you can tell whether we'll be going or not. If the wind's dropped enough, and it's dry, we'll come for you on the ebb tide – three-ish. Yes?'

I nod. 'What do I need to bring?'

'Waterproofs, boots – if you've got them. You'll get wet in any case.'

On the way back I stop to check my phone when I get to the hilly bit. There's one bar of signal: I wait for my messages to flash up, but there aren't any. Not one. Not even from my sisters or Molly, my friend from school. The urge to send one to Sam is so strong it's all I can do to stop myself. Is he allowed to have his phone

71

with him? I don't even know that. But I promised myself I wouldn't phone him first . . .

Now I'm remembering a happy time, under the tree in the park near his nan's house, about a week before he passed his driving test. Early June, hot and sunny in the late afternoon. I'm lying with my head on his chest, we're both dozing in the heat. I open my eyes, and for a second I can't work out what I'm seeing. Leaves falling? Petals? But no, it's white butterflies, hundreds of them, as if they've just hatched out from their chrysalises, and they are floating and spinning in the sunlight that filters through the tree. 'Look, Sam!' I say, and he opens his eyes and watches them with me. And then he sits up and leans over my face and he kisses me, and all around us the air is full of fluttering white wings.

A tree full of white butterflies.

A long, soft kiss.

It's the most romantic thing that has ever happened to me.

I didn't tell anyone about it; not even Molly. And I'm glad now, seeing what happened after.

Ten

Hebrides
Southwesterly
gale force 8 expected later.
Sea state rough
or very rough.
Occasional rain or showers.
Visibility moderate or good,
occasionally poor.

Hebrides
Gale warning.
Southwesterly
gale force 8, veering west,
severe gale 9 to 10,
violent storm.
Rain, then squally showers.
Visibility poor,
becoming moderate.

Hebrides
Westerly
veering southwest 6 to 7,
gale 8 expected later.
Rain.

Eleven

The storm lasts three days. Rain and wind batter the house. The sea is slate-grey, the waves lashed with white. We light the peat stove in the sitting room: it feels like winter. The cloud is so low you can't see more than a few metres out to sea; the windows fog up and even the air inside the house feels salty damp.

We're cooped up in the house watching DVDs and reading all that time. Dad's the only one who goes anywhere further than the shop: he puts on all his wet-weather gear and walks through driving rain to the hides on the loch, to see what rare birds have been blown in by the gales.

Sunday morning, I wake to a pale blue cloudless sky framed in the skylight windows, and the oddest thing: silence.

No wind.

We are bound to go today, aren't we? I listen to the shipping forecast just in case, like Finn said. I've heard it so often these last three days I'm starting to know the names of the places, and what the different things mean: wind, sea state, weather, visibility. They do it in the same order each time.

Dad listens too. He says he likes the sounds of the words: *a litany of names. Rockall, Malin, Hebrides* . . . He recites a poem to me, by Carol Ann Duffy, which has some of the names in it. Only *Finisterre* isn't one of the places in the shipping forecast any more.

'Since 2002,' Dad says. 'Now they call it Fitzroy. It's because there are two places called Finisterre and that might get confusing for sailors.' He smiles at me. 'Finisterre is much more poetic, don't you think? It means *land's end* or *the end of the earth*. The *end of the world* even.'

I shrug.

'Anyway, since when have you been so interested in the shipping forecast, Kate?'

'Finn's going to take me to find cockles,' I say. 'But only when the weather's good.'

'In a boat?'

'Yes,' I say. 'But he's very experienced. It's only a rowing boat. We won't be going far.'

Dad narrows his eyes. 'How far *exactly*?'

My heart sinks.

'Show me on the map,' Dad says.

But I've forgotten the name of the island now. Not sure that Finn ever told me. 'I don't know,' I say. 'I'll ask him when he comes to collect me.'

'Which is when?'

'When the tide turns. You collect cockles on an ebb tide.'

Mum's listening from the table where she's writing postcards. She smiles. 'Hark at you!' she says. 'Quite the island girl already.'

'Shut up, Mum!'

It takes me a while to work out why I suddenly feel so cross.

Island girl. Of course. The pretty girl at the lobster house. Will she be coming too?

The morning drags. I don't dare go anywhere in case they come for me earlier than I expect. Mum and Dad make a picnic and set off on a walk together. 'Be sure to leave us a note,' Mum says, 'with all the details. Where you are going and when you are coming back.'

I watch them go off, side by side, but not holding hands or anything. The sun's out. Mum's wearing a sleeveless T-shirt and jeans. Her hair's loose. She looks younger. I hear her laugh at something Dad says.

I'm watching from the window when the jeep turns up. Piers is driving; Thea opens her door and jumps down from the front passenger seat.

I pull on my boots and grab my bag and open the front door. 'Coming!' I call.

Thea pushes the seat down so I can scramble into the back.

And there *she* is. But no sign of Finn.

Thea introduces us. 'Isla, Kate.'

'Hello,' the girl says. A soft, island accent. Auburn hair, pale, flawless skin, shiny blue-green eyes.

'Well, we've got our perfect day at last,' Thea says. 'It's been awful the last few days, hasn't it? The worst summer storm I can remember!' She and Piers chatter away in the front. Isla and I sit quietly in the back. The jeep bumps and jolts and I have to concentrate on not falling against her when the road bends or Piers swerves to avoid a sheep.

I pluck up courage to ask about Finn. 'Is he ill?'

Thea laughs. 'No! Sorry. Assumed you would know. We're meeting Finn at the boat, just to save time. He's getting everything ready. Like he usually does.'

Isla smiles. Of course, she'd know.

'What's the name of the place we're going?' I ask.

'The island's called Collay. No one lives there now. Only sheep.'

Too late, I remember about leaving a note for Mum.

We have to wade out to get into the boat. Water slops over the top of my boots, so from the start I've got soggy feet. Finn holds the rope (the *painter*, he calls it) with one hand, and with the other, helps each of us to balance as we clamber in. He wades out, pushing the boat and at the last minute he climbs in. The boat wobbles and I squeal. Can't stop myself.

Piers and Finn take an oar each. They sit on the seat in the middle; Isla goes forward to the front with the buckets and rake, and Thea and I sit in the back. It's a squash. We seem to be horribly low in the water. Every time the oars lift they send drips of water flicking back over me and Thea.

The sea is like a millpond. Pale blue, and the sky a milky kind of blue too. Birds fly low over the water ahead of us. It's unbelievably beautiful in the stillness and quiet. The movement is mesmerising; the rhythmic stroke of the oars, the gentle movement over small waves. Already the beach looks a long way behind us. Further out there's more breeze, but not much, not enough to whip up waves or anything scary. It's hazy ahead. Gradually the shape of the island comes into view, and Finn and Piers row harder, pulling across the current, to get to the flat beach where we'll land. No one speaks. It's as if we are all under some kind of spell.

The pale strip of sand becomes wider as we get nearer, the tide ebbing fast. I trail my hand in the clear sea. I can see the bottom as clearly as looking through glass. Green weed like flowing grass, and thicker brown flat weed: the kelp the seals love, Finn says. Small silvery fish in shoals dart away from my hand. A bright orange starfish moves slowly along the seabed. The water gets shallower: nearly there. Isla gets ready with the rope, and when Finn calls out she slides herself off the boat and wades through the shallows, pulling us in. She knows exactly what to do. I guess she's done it hundreds of times before.

We all pile out of the boat. Finn and Piers haul it in, up the beach and fasten the rope under a stone.

Piers hands me a bucket. 'See here?' He rakes the sand at the edge of the water and bends down to scoop up a handful of cream-coloured shells. 'This is what we are looking for. Choose the bigger ones.'

So. Cockles turn out to be these ordinary-looking shells, creamy white and honey coloured, only they are still alive, with the two halves tight together. *Bivalves*, Piers calls them. There are hundreds of them, slightly buried under the sand.

We set to work, scooping them up in handfuls and dropping them in the buckets of sea water to keep them fresh.

'Delicious cooked with leeks and garlic and white wine,' Piers says.

I still can't imagine eating them.

Isla is quicker than me. She doesn't seem to get backache from the bending and scooping like I do. I have to keep stretching my back out, to ease my spine. After a while I've had enough. My hands are numb.

'Why don't you go and explore the island for a bit?' Thea suggests. 'Collecting cockles is back-breaking if you're not used to it. And seeing as it's your first time on Collay, you should have a look round. We'll have some tea later. We brought cake.'

I walk slowly up the beach. My feet squelch with every step. I pull off my boots and socks and walk barefoot instead. The sand is white, sparkling in the sunlight with fragments of silvery crystal. I abandon my wet boots, spread my socks over flat rocks at the top of the beach and walk on.

It's like a miniature version of our island: a fringe of beaches, short grass studded with little flowers, a carpet of pink and white and yellow. Bees. Flocks of small brown birds. Sheep. No roads though, and no houses except ruined ones: tumbledown stones covered with nettles and taller grass and other weeds. I climb to the top of the island, sit on an outcrop of rock. From here I can see down to the beach, and the small figures of the others, bending, scooping, the shells clattering against each other in the bucket. They look as if they are working in a kind of rhythm. They could be from any time at all. Like centuries back. I screw up my eyes to see better against the brightness. Finn and Isla work side by side, slowly moving along through the shallow water, slightly apart from Piers and Thea. I wonder what they are talking about. If they are talking. I try not to mind how close they look.

The misty, milky sky seems to cut Collay off totally: you can't see the other islands at all. I close my eyes, listen to the birds and the sea and the bees humming all around. It's bliss to feel warm sun on my face and arms after so many days of rain. Voices drift up.

When I next look, Thea's getting things out of a basket on the rocks near my boots. I make my way slowly back down to join them for tea and cake.

'We should start back, soon,' Finn says.

'Why are the houses all ruined?' I say. 'What happened?'

'Same as on lots of the other islands,' Finn says. 'Too harsh living out here in the winter, cut off for days and weeks even. Too small to grow enough food for a family to be self-sufficient.'

'It would be amazing to stay overnight though,' Piers says. 'We should come over and camp when the others get here.'

'Are the sheep wild?' I ask.

Isla smiles. 'No. They're brought over by boat in the early summer, and collected in the autumn: they spend the winter back on the inhabited isles.'

I try to imagine it: ferrying sheep in a small boat across the water. Like *why*?

'The grazing here is particularly good,' Isla explains, as if she knows what I'm thinking. 'Crofters have grazing rights on lots of the uninhabited islands. But most don't bother these days.'

Finn watches her as she talks.

Her face is pink from the sun. Her hair's coming undone from where she's looped it up with a slide; golden-red tendrils curling round her neck. She is really pretty, but in her own way, nothing like the girls back home. No make-up. Old, faded cotton T-shirt and skirt. I wonder how old she is. She's both shy and confident at the same time, if that's possible. Like she's quiet, but she knows stuff. Knows who she is. She's natural and easy with the boat. No wonder Finn likes her.

'Jamie and Tim and the others will be arriving on the ferry in the morning,' Piers says. He glances at Isla. She blushes slightly.

Finn looks away.

Piers goes on. 'Two days late, because of the storm. The ferry couldn't land.'

The sea is creeping up the beach, lapping at the boat. Thea packs up the remainder of the cake. 'Come on, time to go.'

The air has already cooled down. It's colder still once we've left the shelter of the bay and are heading

82

back across the water. Isla takes a turn at rowing; I go forward in the boat so Piers can sit with Thea at the back. The boat rocks alarmingly as we swap places.

I watch Finn and Isla. They are perfectly synchronised, rowing together, sitting side by side with their backs to me. They lean forwards, lifting the oars, dipping and drawing them back. Drips of water fly off the oars like liquid pearls.

Mist rises off the water. Everyone's silent the whole way back.

I don't stay for supper, even though Thea invites me to. I walk back alone along the road. As I come into the village, I can see someone in the red telephone kiosk. I know instantly it's Dad. His tall frame, awkwardly crushed into the small space, talking into the old black phone, running his other hand through his hair. He's talking fast, intently: he has no idea I can see him.

He could be talking to anyone. Like Bonnie, or Granny, or someone from work . . .

But my heart sinks. The way he looks, even though I can't hear a word of what he's saying: it's all so horribly obvious he's talking to a woman, to someone he cares about, who is missing him . . .

I feel sick to the core.

Twelve

On the face of it, everything looks all right. It's sunny for the next couple of days; Mum and Dad go out together for walks; they take food with them for picnics. They go on a boat trip and return flushed from sun and the wind, full of stories about the birds they saw, and the basking sharks they watched from the boat on the way back.

I half wish I'd gone with them. Except that I've got that horrible sick feeling in the pit of my stomach all the time now. I can't stop thinking about what Dad might have been saying down the phone line. My mind worries at it, imagining the sordid details, the words he might have been saying.

Just wait a bit longer; as soon as this holiday is over I can be with you again.

Of course, I would rather be with you than stuck on this island with them . . .

I had to do this, to be sure. But spending this time with her makes me realise that it's all over . . .

*Kate's old enough now ... children are resil-
ient ... she'll be fine ...*

Does Mum know? Is she full of worry and dread
too? Surely she's guessed something? Or perhaps
they're coming to some sort of agreement. He'll
leave, she'll have the house ... Perhaps she's
seeing someone?

Why don't you ask them straight out? That's what
my friend Molly would say. But Molly hasn't a clue.
Her parents are happy together. Her family talk about
everything openly. But we've never been like that. If
Sam and I were still seeing each other, I could tell him
about it. If Sam and I were together, maybe none of
this would feel so important ...

Only I know that's not true. Not really.

Everything − my whole world − is in the balance,
about to tip.

I make myself remember happy times.

Christmas, Hannah's first year at uni. We rented
a cottage in Northumberland with Molly's family. It
didn't snow, but it was freezing cold. Temperatures
plummeted every night, and hoar frost furred every
twig and stem, almost as thick as snow. The paths
and lane were iced to a slippery polish. We walked
on Christmas morning in thick white mist, Dad and
Molly's dad leading the way, using their navigation
skills and the map and compass, and we got hope-
lessly lost, and everyone laughed and it didn't
matter. Not one bit. Mum and Molly's mum and
Hannah cooked Christmas dinner and there was

nearly a disaster when the duck fat got too hot and the kitchen was full of smoke but Mum just laughed and laughed and we had to open all the windows and doors and we froze for about two hours, but the meal turned out fine and Molly's dad cleaned the oven and everything got sorted. After dinner we played silly games and turned off the lights so we could sit with candles and the light from the fire and everyone was relaxed and happy. Mum and Dad cuddled together on the sofa. Dad sang Mum a song he'd written . . .

It's nice remembering that. Dad, writing songs . . . Dad, happy. Mum's face glowing in the firelight . . .

Or that summer we went to the beach in Wales, where Dad climbed down the cliff quicker than everyone else, so that as the rest of us came over the edge of the hill we looked down and saw the words he had written in the sand: *I LOVE YOU!*

It was the most romantic thing we'd ever seen him do for Mum. She had tears in her eyes.

But that was all years ago. It hasn't been like that for a long, long time.

The squeal of bike brakes makes me look up. Finn's skidded to a stop outside the house. I jump up, check my face quickly to make sure he can't tell I've been crying, and go to the door.

'Hello, you! Busy?' he asks.

My face goes hot. It's so obvious I'm not doing anything. Wasting my day.

'Want to come and help get the peat? Everyone's

coming. You can meet them all. Tim and Jamie and the others.'

I nod. 'OK.'

'It'll be hard work, mind.'

He's remembering what I was like with the cockle picking.

'I'll do my best,' I say. 'I'm not used to it, that's all. Not like your *Isla*.'

Her name slips out before I've really thought. He gives me a funny look. 'She's not mine,' he says very quietly.

'Sorry,' I say quickly. 'I know I'm rubbish at practical things.'

'Stop that,' Finn says. 'You're just fine, Kate. Stop putting yourself down.'

Tears well up again. I turn my head so he can't see, grab my scarf and a jacket from the hooks in the hall.

Is that what I do? I wonder. *Put myself down?*

'I'll give you a backie if you like,' Finn says.

'A what?'

'A ride on the back of the bike. It'll be quicker that way.'

'Oh! Yes, OK.'

He waits for me to clamber on behind him. 'Hold on tight!' he says. 'It's a bit of a bumpy ride. And you'll have to get off for the hill.'

We wobble along through the village, me trying to balance and laughing so much I nearly fall off. I have to walk the next bit, which is uphill. The very last bit is the best: a long freewheel down the track to the

Manse. At the bottom, the bike slows, stops and I get off. I can't stop smiling.

Finn grins. 'You should get yourself a bike!' he says. 'You'd really enjoy it. You could get around the whole island then, and see the best places.'

'Mum hired one from the man at the garage,' I tell him. 'But it was rubbish. Old and cranky and she got a puncture.'

'We might have one you could borrow,' Finn says. 'We'll look in the shed later.'

Alex waves from the door of the Manse. I wave back. Piers and Thea are putting tools into the back of the jeep. A dark-haired, good-looking bloke in a tweed jacket and jeans is leaning against the stone wall, a mug of coffee in one hand which he raises as if in greeting.

'That's Tim,' Finn says. 'Jamie and Clara are somewhere around too.' He waves vaguely in the direction of the house.

'We won't all fit in the jeep,' I say. Duh! Obviously.

'No. So you and I can go on the bike, and the others will walk up.'

'What do we have to do exactly?'

'Piers and I will finish cutting the peat. You can help shift the stuff that's already been cut and dried; put the peats in sacks so we can bring them back down in the jeep. Then we build the proper peat stack next to the house. I'll show you: there's a special way to do it, so the peats can dry out and then make a weatherproof skin to last the winter.'

'It sounds complicated,' I say.

'Not really. It's easier if everyone helps. It'll be fun. You'll see.'

Everyone's quite a lot older than us. Finn isn't intimidated like me, but that's because he knows them all and, in any case, he's the one who seems to know the most about the peat and the traditional ways to do things, more than his older brothers even.

Piers and Thea climb into the jeep.

'Here's Jamie and Clara,' Finn says. 'Come and say hello.'

Jamie's a rounder, more solid version of Piers, with fairer, curlier hair. Clara is petite and gorgeous, with short fair hair and almond-shaped eyes like a pixie.

'This is Kate,' Finn tells them. 'She's staying at Fiona's place for the summer.'

'Hi,' Clara says. 'Nice to meet you, Kate.'

Jamie nods but doesn't say anything.

'We'll see you up there,' Finn says.

We climb back on the bike. But it's too difficult to pedal uphill with me: we walk the long way back up the slope until the track levels out again.

This part of the island is covered in springy heather, humming with bees. There are silvery trails of water between black banks of peaty soil, pools reflecting sky. Now, ahead of us, I can see lines of people working at the peat banks. Finn's smiling, waving. 'Isn't it wonderful?' he says to me. 'To think we're doing the exact same work that's been done on the island for hundreds of years. Except in the old days people would have horses and carts rather than jeeps and cars, of course.'

I think of Mum, at the garden centre, choosing compost. 'I thought we were running out of peat?' I say. 'Like you're not supposed to buy it for gardening any more.'

'That's totally different. Yes, it's terrible where peat extraction's happened on a huge mechanical scale, like in parts of Ireland. But this is small scale, sustainable, hand-cutting for one family's domestic use. It's like the difference between small scale fishing in a little family boat, versus those vile enormous trawlers with dredge nets that bring up everything off the seabed.'

'OK, OK,' I say quickly before he goes on. 'Sorry. I guess I'm just pig ignorant.'

He gives me a look. 'Stop it!'

'I know, I'm doing it again. It's a habit.'

'A bad one!'

Tim's really efficient: he does most of the heavy carrying, lifting the sacks up into the back of the jeep. The rest of us fill the sacks, but talking and larking about at the same time. Piers recites a poem by some Irish poet; he tells me about the Tollund man, found perfectly preserved in a Danish peat bog. Finn works the hardest, of course, cutting a new line of fresh peat with the specially designed spade. Piers and Jamie follow behind, digging the peat and stacking it up. Piers sings at the top of his voice and Jamie joins in. They don't care in the slightest what anyone thinks. They're enjoying themselves too much.

'Are you having a good holiday?' Tim asks, as he waits for me to fill up a sack.

'Yes.' I realise I almost *am*, in spite of everything. 'Though it's not at all how I imagined it would be.'

He heaves the sack up and dumps it in the jeep. 'What did you imagine?'

'I don't know. I had no idea the island was going to be this small, and remote, and so different from anywhere I've ever been. *Remember* being,' I correct myself. 'I was here as a baby. And I suppose I didn't imagine meeting people . . . making new friends. Doing stuff like this and actually enjoying it!'

'You're here with your family?'

'Mum and Dad. Not my sisters. They're older . . . they're doing their own thing this summer. Well, Hannah's working.'

He listens while I talk about them. He has gorgeous brown eyes. He's incredibly handsome. I wonder what Bonnie or Hannah would think.

I find myself telling him more than I meant to, little by little.

'The worst thing is that my parents are on the verge of splitting up. The holiday was supposed to make things better, but it hasn't. If anything, it's made it worse.' I blink back tears.

Tim puts his arm round my shoulders and hugs me. 'I'm sorry, Kate.'

I wriggle away, embarrassed.

He doesn't take any notice. 'That's harsh. It really is. But you'll be OK. Really. It's happened to so many of us. Thea. Me. It gets easier, believe me. You'll find that too, given time. But it is very hard to begin with. I understand that.'

I look over at Thea, smiling at something Jamie's just said. *You can't tell*, I'm thinking. *No one would know from the outside. Tim, even!* I don't know why that comes as a surprise to me, but it does. For me, it's like this horrible shameful thing, as if it's my fault, a weakness in me, something I should have been able to stop . . .

But I can't say any of that out loud. Not to Tim, not to anyone.

Tim's still talking. 'And the best thing to do is to keep busy. Don't think about it too much. So let's get that next sack filled and into the jeep.'

Piers starts reciting lines from another poem: 'Wordsworth's *The Solitary Reaper*,' he announces pompously. Jamie and Clara join in.

Tim pulls a face and makes me laugh, despite everything.

Back at the Manse, Finn goes straight up to have a bath. So I look after myself. I go along the bookcases, searching for a copy of Wordsworth's poems. I find the one they were chanting up on the peat beds about the Highland girl singing. I copy my two favourite lines into my notebook:

> *Breaking the silence of the seas*
> *Among the farthest Hebrides.*

Piers smiles when he sees what I'm reading. 'I'll find you the Heaney poems about the Bog People too,' he says.

No one thinks it's the least bit odd that I'm curled up with a book and a cup of tea, reading poetry. I guess this is how they live all the time. Joy brings in freshly baked cake: fruit tea-bread, and ginger cake with sticky bits. 'For the workers,' she says. 'Tuck in. You've all done a great job and I'm very thankful. Now we can heat the Manse all winter.'

I wonder what Dad would say if he saw me here, like this. Pleased, I guess, that at last I'm showing some interest in *poetry*. And Mum? She'd be envious, more likely, of the company. Like when she talked about watching Finn's family and friends on the beach, years ago. *It looked fun*, she said, in that wistful tone. As if she'd wished she could be part of it too.

How isolated Mum and Dad have become. How strange that I've not noticed till now how almost all their friends have drifted away . . .

Finn hasn't reappeared after his bath, and as I'm here as his guest, it makes me feel a bit odd. Should I go home now? But no one seems to be bothered about me still being here, and it's cosy and friendly and much nicer than walking back to the house, not knowing what I'll find when I get there.

Eventually Alex and Joy invite me to stay for supper, so I do. Finn comes downstairs at last. He doesn't pay me any particular attention. Tim does though. He makes sure I feel at home. He sits next to me and chats about his job in publishing. He's a sales representative, selling books to supermarkets. He travels all the time.

He's grown-up, with a proper job and a flat and a car and everything, but he's kind, not scary or showing off how clever he is, like the others do a bit. Not Finn, I don't mean, because he's not clever-clever in an academic way. Though the way Finn talks about the island, it sometimes seems a bit like he's lecturing me . . .

'I can take you home after dinner if you like,' Tim says.

Thea looks up: she watches us for a while.

Tim notices her watching. 'Want to come with me to take Kate home?' he asks her.

She shakes her head. 'Ask Finn,' she says.

But he's busy, it seems. Other things to do. Perhaps it's just a signal to me: that he's not interested in me *that* way. It feels a bit like a snub, but I know I am *overly sensitive* about these things. So Molly always says.

It's actually rather nice being driven by Tim in his big estate car. He drives slowly and carefully: very different from Piers. He talks a bit more about his work. He drives around the country selling books. He's travelled all over the world, but he loves it here on this island more than anywhere else, even the most exotic places.

'Really?' I say. 'What, even more than the Seychelles or the Caribbean?'

'Yes!' he says. 'Even more than those.'

The car bumps over the cattle grid. Tim carries on talking. 'How about you? What job might you do when you grow up, Kate?'

Those two little words – *grow up* – make me cringe. He thinks I'm just a child.

'I've no idea,' I say. 'It's too hard to know what I could do. Like there must be loads of jobs I haven't even heard of. I don't know how you find out.' I look at him. 'Did you always know what you wanted to be?'

He laughs as if I've said something hilarious. 'A life-long ambition to be a sales rep, you mean?'

I shrug.

'No,' he says. 'I wanted to be a writer or a broadcast journalist.'

'And do you still?'

He looks at me, still faintly amused. 'Well, of course. You don't stop dreaming, just because you've grown up! Haven't your parents told you that?'

'No,' I say. 'They don't tell me anything.'

That shuts him up. And in any case we've arrived, and he's parking up on the grassy verge near the house. 'I'm sorry,' he says, when the engine's stopped. He puts his hand on my shoulder lightly. 'I touched a raw nerve. I didn't mean to upset you.'

'I'm not upset,' I lie. 'Thanks for the lift.' I shut the car door and walk away quickly.

Dad's in his usual seat at the window. He looks as if he's about to say something, but I go straight upstairs before he can.

I lie on my bed. Stare through the low window at the framed square of sea, rock, grass, sky. Gradually I calm down.

*　　*　　*

95

I know a bit about what Dad's dreams used to be because of what Mum told me the other day when we were on the beach. And Mum? She wanted lots of children: the family she didn't have as a child. I remember her telling me ages ago that for a while she'd thought of having her own business ... something like a community family centre, where people could come together to play and meet each other, with a café and a toys and books library, and classes for children and adults to learn how to make things, or dance or play music. Only she couldn't work out how to earn money that way.

And what about me, and my dreams?

All I ever wanted was for Mum and Dad to sort things out and stay together. Us be a family. Just for things to be OK. It didn't seem much to ask.

I did have this silly fantasy about Sam and me, once upon a time, going off together on some kind of adventure: travelling, I suppose, seeing the world and meeting different kinds of people – I was a bit vague about the details. Sam was always talking about getting away – being *free*. I didn't think about *how* you get to do those things, about how you pay for them, or any of the practical stuff. I didn't ever tell Sam about it even. It seems ridiculous now.

Thirteen

I've just finished breakfast when I see Finn through the front window, riding his bike up the track towards our house, one hand on the saddle of a second bike. The spare bike. I'm touched he remembered.

I open the front door and step out on to the grass. It's sunny, the air not warm exactly, but sweet and delicious.

'Delivery of one bike.' He smiles as he dismounts and wheels both bikes across the grass.

'Doesn't anyone else want to use it? You've got all those visitors now,' I say.

'Your need is as great as theirs. Greater even,' Finn says.

I frown slightly. 'Why's that?'

'No car at your disposal. All alone with no friends at your house for instant entertainment . . .'

'Yeah, all right. No need to rub it in! Billy-no-mates, you mean!'

Finn smiles. 'Why don't you get your stuff and come with me for a bike ride right now?'

'OK!' I grab my jacket from the hooks by the door, shove my feet into trainers. 'Where, exactly? Mum will want to know. I keep getting into trouble for not telling them.'

'To the beaches on the west coast. So bring your swimming things. We'll go via Isla's house and see if she wants to come too.'

That changes everything. I'm disappointed, and cross with myself that I am, both at the same time. It's not as if I fancy Finn, is it?

Do I?

I run back upstairs to find my swimming things. I hesitate, put back the sensible black costume and pick up my peacock blue bikini.

By the time I've got back outside, Mum's there chatting to Finn. Of course she likes him. She's probably relieved I'm spending time with a boy like that instead of moping over Sam. But does she have to be so obvious about it?

'I'm ready. Shall we go?' I say to Finn.

'Have a lovely time,' Mum says. 'It's a perfect day for the beach. I'm almost tempted to join you.'

I get on the bike quickly before Finn gets any ideas about inviting her along too.

Finn cycles next to me so we can talk as we bowl along. 'She's nice, your mum. She seems happy enough. Are things going better with her and your dad?'

'It's hard to tell. They are speaking, and doing walks and things together.'

'That's good, isn't it?'

'I don't know. I think it's maybe too late.'

Dad, at the phone box.

We cycle on another three miles or so, round the big curve of the bay, as far as the turning to Isla's house. 'I'll wait here,' I tell Finn. 'Catch my breath.'

'She might not be in,' Finn says. 'I'll go and see.'

He takes ages. I sit on the top of a wooden field gate to wait. The sky's a thin, transparent blue with streaks of fine white cloud. The wind's blowing as usual, rustling the tall grasses. The sound of the sea has become so familiar to me I hardly notice it now, but it's there all the time, more of a murmur than a roar today. A flock of little birds take off, windblown as they get higher: you can see them struggling and then giving in, going where the wind takes them, and dropping down into another area of thistles in the field of barley.

It's beginning to look so much more beautiful to me, this island landscape, than it did when we first arrived. The wide expanses of sky. How wild and untamed it seems, even though I know people have lived and farmed here for hundreds of years. Thousands, even. I can understand better why Finn wants it all to stay this way for ever. Why he's so opposed to change, to the wind farm . . .

Voices. Two bikes come into view. Finn's face is flushed with happiness.

'Hello, Kate,' Isla says in her soft, lilting voice as they get nearer. 'It's a beautiful day. I'm glad you're getting to see the island at its best.'

The three of us cycle together, Isla in the middle. We go quite fast: I'm pleased I can keep up despite not having had much practice. No doubt Isla cycles everywhere all the time. Her bike is old and she doesn't have gears, but you hardly need them. We only see two cars the whole way.

The road peters out and becomes a track. It gets narrower and goes uphill, then stops altogether. The wind's stronger: a westerly blowing in across the Atlantic. We park up the bikes. Finn padlocks them together.

'Why?' Isla says. 'There's absolutely no need, Finn. No one's going to steal a bike!'

'Better to be sure,' he says. 'It's not just islanders here in the summer. There are tourists, visitors. So you can't really know.'

'Three men from the wind farm project arrived on the ferry yesterday,' Isla says. 'They're staying at Martinstown. They are hoping to *win hearts and minds*, Dad says, with the new exhibition at the hall.'

Finn frowns. 'Not again!'

She looks out to sea. 'You'd see it all really clearly from here.'

'You'd see it wherever you were on the island,' Finn says. 'Daytime, and even more so at night. Hear it too.'

Isla looks at him. 'I don't think so, not above the sound of the wind and the waves. But you would see it, you're right about that. It would change this view for ever.'

'Not just the view. It would change everything,' Finn says. 'We've got to do something, Isla. Make people wake up and understand what's at stake. It's not right that everyone with a vested interest gets a voice and we don't.'

'But we do. That was the whole point of the public consultation,' Isla says. 'And quite a lot of the islanders are in favour. They think we have to move with the times. It'll bring jobs: the construction, and maintenance, servicing, all those sort of things. It will bring business here. It might mean young people can actually stay on the island and find work, instead of having to leave for the mainland.'

'You sound as if you actually believe all that!' Finn says.

'I'm trying to be fair. We have to listen to what everyone wants. It's easy for you to say you want things to stay exactly as they are. You don't have to make a living here. Islanders have a long history of having to adapt and change.'

I listen to them argue, back and forth.

Isla's good, I have to admit. Plus, she has the trump card of being born here, living here all the time.

Finn has no answer to that.

'Shall we go down to the beach?' I say eventually. 'Which way?'

Isla leads. I notice how light she is on her feet; her easy, graceful way of walking. Halfway along, she stops to take off her shoes and walk barefoot over the peaty ground. 'Try it,' she says to me. 'It feels delicious. The soles of your feet are as sensitive as your hands, did you know that?'

Finn waits while I take my trainers off, but he keeps his own firmly laced up. Isla has gone ahead. The wind blows her thin cotton skirt against her legs, whips her long hair sideways. She fits perfectly here, as if she's just a part of the landscape. The same colours even: blue and gold.

Finn's watching her too, and the expression on his face is one of longing, and pain. He's in love with her. But she doesn't love him back.

It's obvious to me now.

We come down the cliff. The beaches I've seen already have been beautiful in a vast, windswept kind of way, but this one is totally stunning, like something in a holiday advert for a tropical paradise. This must be what Tim meant, yesterday. White sand, turquoise sea, framed by arms of rock stretching round on either side. It's almost deserted: one small family group have made a camp at the top of the beach.

Isla's already running across the sand, spinning round with her arms out. She looks so joyous and free and wild I can't help joining in too. 'Isn't it the most beautiful beach you have ever seen?' she says, eyes shining. 'Let's swim while the sun's out.'

We undress quickly, pulling on our swimming things. We leave our clothes in a neat pile.

'Put a big pebble on top,' Isla says, 'to stop the wind blowing them away.'

She is slim and pale-skinned; in her pale green swimming costume she looks amazing, but you can tell she doesn't even think about how she looks to anyone else. It's just not on her radar.

'It'll be freezing,' she says. 'You just have to run in and dive under straight away. But it'll be worth it.'

Finn's walking along the beach vaguely in our direction, but not looking at us. Every so often he bends over to pick up a pebble or a shell or something.

'Should we wait for Finn?' I say.

'No!' Isla laughs. 'Now he's in a mood I bet he won't swim. Come on,' and she grabs my hand and starts to run, pulling me with her.

The cold takes my breath away. Isla hangs on to my hand, pulling me in deeper, until we both fall, laughing and screeching into the waves. We start to swim, but the waves are breaking right over us and we end up half bouncing, half swimming until we're through the breaking foam and out into deeper water. She swims like a seal; strong and confident. I swim parallel to the shore, not going out too far, a bit nervous of the waves. I'm exhausted and numb with cold long before she is, and I wade back out, shivering, with purple gooseflesh thighs and arms, and hair in rat's tails.

I run up the beach to my towel. There's no sign of Finn.

It's too cold to stay in a wet bikini a second longer than I have to. I dry myself quickly and struggle back into my clothes and my teeth are still chattering.

Isla joins me. 'Wasn't that brilliant?' she says, shaking with cold. 'Aren't you glad you braved it?'

'Sort of!' I say. 'But it was totally freezing. I can't imagine ever going in again.'

She pulls her jumper over her head and starts drying her hair.

'Have a rummage in my bag,' she says, chucking it over. 'I brought us tea.'

I find the flask. 'Wow. Amazing.' It's the sort of thing Mum would do; bring a hot drink for after swimming. We take turns to sip from the cup. My toes and hands begin to thaw. The blood rushes to my face; I'm tingling all over. 'Now, it feels good!' I tell Isla.

'Is he often in a mood?' I ask her. We're both watching Finn walking slowly along at the far end of the beach.

'Only since this business with the wind farm,' Isla says. 'It's really upsetting him. But he's got a bit of a fantasy about island life. It's because he's just here in his school holidays. Plus his parents are wealthy; they don't have to worry about work and earning money or anything real.'

'He told me he'd like to live here all the time,' I say. 'And he intends to, when he's finished with school.'

She sighs impatiently. 'Yes, but what will he do, exactly? He can't just sponge off his parents, can he? He's just not being realistic.'

'Rich people have this way of making money out of money they've already got. Like they buy houses and rent them out, or they invest in business and stuff, don't they? So they don't have to do a job like ordinary people.'

Isla frowns. 'It's not right. It's no way to live. Working connects you to where you live, to the other people around. Everyone should contribute to their community in some way: that's what I think.'

'But it all depends on the kind of work you do,' I say. 'I mean, there are awful jobs. For some people it's not much better than slavery. Rubbish pay, terrible hours and conditions. No satisfaction or pleasure in it at all.'

She looks at me. 'Well, yes. That's all true too.'

'What will you do?' I ask her.

'I'll do my exams here and then I'll go to college on the mainland to train to be a midwife. When I'm qualified, I'll come back to the island as a community midwife. That's my plan.'

I'm quiet for a while.

'You look sad,' Isla says, out of the blue.

'Just thinking,' I say. 'Wishing I knew what I wanted, like you do.'

'You've got plenty of time,' she says. 'You're younger than me, aren't you?'

'I'm fifteen,' I say.

'Well, then. There's no rush.'

'Maybe if I had plans for my own future I wouldn't worry so much about what's happening with my parents.'

She glances at me, then looks quickly away. She doesn't ask me anything more. It's slightly odd. Most people would have asked what I meant, wouldn't they?

Would want to help even? Or at least say something comforting.

We sit in silence for a while, staring at the sea.

'What's it like, living here all year round?' I ask her.

'It's just normal life; I've never known anything else,' she says. 'I suppose it's quiet by your standards; we don't have shops or clubs or cinemas. But there are ferries to the mainland for all that. And we get films at the community centre. There are parties and ceilidhs.' She smiles. 'Your face!'

'What about it?'

'Disapproving.'

'No!' I say. 'I don't disapprove. Not really. It's just different from what I'm used to.'

'Here, everyone knows you and you know them: it feels safe, in a good way. The weather's important, always, because it affects everything. But I like that. The electricity goes off sometimes when it's windy, but it's no big deal. School's much the same too, only a bit smaller, so you know everyone.' She looks at me. 'What did you think I'd say?'

I shrug. 'I don't know. I suppose I just can't imagine being stuck so far away from everything.'

'It's not far away, if you're here!' She laughs. 'You just need to reset your compass. If this is your actual home, this is the centre of the world.'

I think about that for a bit.

'Anyway,' she says, 'there's the airport. We're not totally cut off. And telly and phones and internet. It's not the dark ages.'

'*My* mobile doesn't work,' I say. 'Only if I climb up the hill above the village, and then only sometimes.'

'You've got the wrong network,' she says. 'That's all.'

Finn comes back and sits down with us, spreads out his treasure of pebbles and shells and feathers on the dry sand. He's found a skull too: a bird of some kind, possibly a tern, he says, tiny and light.

I try to imagine what he could do if he lived all the time on the island: work as a naturalist, perhaps, or a warden on the nature reserve, or in that tiny museum? But you probably have to have a science or history degree before you can do anything like that, and I can't see Finn spending years away at university.

He could grow stuff on the croft, and fish for mackerel, and live very simply off the land ... Perhaps that's the kind of life Dad should have chosen, way back, instead of becoming a teacher. Perhaps that's where things went wrong for him, and it's nothing to do with Mum really.

'So. You chickened out of swimming,' I say to Finn.

'I'm going in now, actually. Do you want to swim again?'

'No way! It was absolutely freezing.'

But Isla does. I almost change my mind when I see her getting changed, and watch Finn and her walking together down to the edge of the sea. She grabs his hand like she did with mine before, and they run into the waves together. I watch them wade out beyond

107

the surf of the breaking waves, start swimming out to sea, their heads two dark dots in the blue.

The dazzle of sunlight reflecting off water makes my eyes ache. I close them. It's warmer, more sheltered, lying down.

I sit up when I hear voices. Lots of people, coming down the path to the beach, talking and laughing, loaded up with bags. They are silhouetted against the sun so it takes a while before I recognise who it is: Piers and Thea and everybody.

Tim waves and comes over. They all follow him, plonking themselves and their bundles of towels, blankets, windbreaks and bags next to me on the sand.

'You here with Finn?' Tim asks.

I nod. 'And Isla. They're swimming.'

Thea and Piers start hammering the windbreak stakes into the sand. They spread out blankets and get boxes of food and drink out of the bags. 'Lunch,' Thea explains. 'Have you had yours?'

'No. I'm not very organised about that sort of thing,' I say.

'Well, help yourself. We brought loads.'

She opens the lid of a tin full of chicken drumsticks, and a plastic tub of salad: proper food. She hands round plates and forks. Bottles of beer. Fresh homemade bread.

Finn and Isla are walking up the beach.

Tim picks up one of the towels and goes towards Isla, wraps her round with it. She smiles at him; he holds her for a second too long.

Finn frowns. He picks up his own towel and rubs his hair. 'Did you see the seals?' he says to me. 'They came right up close to us.'

I shake my head. 'You were too far out for me to see anything.'

Isla takes her clothes with her and goes to find somewhere more private to change. Finn watches her go; he glances at Tim. But Tim's busy tucking into a large plate of chicken and salad as if he's already forgotten all about Isla.

After lunch, everyone lazes in the sun. Even Piers and Jamie are silent. At one point, Tim gets out a notebook and pen and a pair of old-fashioned binoculars. He watches the birds along the edge of the water, makes notes. No one comments: it's just what he does, I suppose. My own notebook stays hidden in the bottom of my bag.

The sky clouds over, mid-afternoon. Thea and Piers pack up the lunch things, Jamie and Clara take down the windbreaks.

'We're planning a party – camping overnight, at another beach,' Tim says. 'Want to come, Kate?'

I look at Finn. His face doesn't give anything away.

'OK. Thanks. When?'

'At the weekend: Saturday night, if the weather's good enough.'

'I don't have a tent or sleeping bag or anything.'

'Doesn't matter. Alex and Joy have one of those huge old canvas things like a marquee and everyone who wants to can sleep in there.'

'We're heading back now,' Thea says. 'See you later, Finn.'

Tim kisses me and Isla goodbye: two kisses, on the cheek. 'Take care,' he says. 'Enjoy the rest of the afternoon.'

Finn ignores him.

'It's Tim's birthday,' Isla explains, once he's gone. 'That's why he's arranging the party.'

'How old will he be?'

'Twenty-three.'

'Ancient,' Finn says. He pokes at the sand with a stick, flicks it at the tiny flies buzzing round the drying seaweed along the tideline.

He's jealous, I think. *Jealous of Tim. About Isla.* It's all becoming clear to me now.

'Let's go back via Martinstown,' Finn says. 'Have a look at that exhibition.'

'What's the point?' Isla says. 'You've already made up your mind.'

'I'll go with you,' I say. 'I'd like to find out more.'

Isla shrugs. 'I need to get back in any case. I'm going out with my dad on the boat at high tide.'

We climb back up the cliff to the bikes and cycle the first bit of the way together before Isla splits off to go home. Finn doesn't say much. We're cycling into the wind: it's hard work. The road is long and straight and exposed.

I've not been to Martinstown before: it's a surprise to see lots of new houses, and a café, a children's playground and a big grey hall: the community centre. It's an ugly building; more like something you'd see on the mainland. There are cars parked along the grass verge. Lights on in the building.

We lock the bikes.

Finn's in a bad mood even before we go inside.

It's crowded with people, talking as they go round the exhibition. I follow Finn round, looking at the stands: big panels of photographs, planning drawings, text. It's all very professional. Like loads of money has been spent on making it look really good. Statistics about the number of jobs that will be created, the benefits the project will bring to the island; even how they plan to stop birds flying into the structures. Seems they've thought of everything.

There are photos of other wind farms, off the northwest coast of England, to show what it will look like. Nothing too bad . . .

But Finn's fuming. 'It's outrageously misleading! These wind farms are tiny compared with what they want to build here! They're totally different constructions, with different bases and everything. The landscapes are completely different too. Those ones are all near places which have had heavy industry before, not somewhere beautiful and unique and unspoilt . . .'

A woman nearby stops to listen to his rant. I recognise her, from the checkout in the village supermarket.

'So what's the alternative?' I ask Finn.

'Find another site, one which won't spoil the lives of a whole community. Or put it much, much further out to sea: properly offshore instead of a couple of measly miles. But it's a million times better to use tidal energy instead of wind – it's much more efficient and reliable. Like the scheme being planned near the Orkneys. That's the proper way forward.'

'They should just go the nuclear route,' the woman says. 'It's the obvious solution to the energy problem. Just get on with it, like they do in France.'

Except even I know that's not right. How can it be? When no one knows how to store the waste safely, and it lasts for thousands and thousands of years? And who would want a nuclear power station to be built near them?

Other people are watching and listening now. An older man says something about jobs for islanders. Finn looks as if he is about to explode.

I tug his arm. 'Can we get a coffee? I'm dying for one.'

I drag him away from the exhibition into the café next-door. 'I'll buy. What do you want? Tea? Coffee? Hot chocolate?' If I keep talking maybe I can stop him really making a scene.

His face is white with anger.

'Get us a window table, Finn,' I say. 'I'll bring the drinks over.'

By the time I'm sitting down with him at the table, his mood has changed. It's as if the fight's gone out of him: now he just seems crumpled, defeated.

I try to come up with something positive, anything to make him cheer up a bit.

'Well, at least lots of people are taking an interest,' I say. 'That hall is packed. So, perhaps people are more open-minded than you think. Now might be a good time to present the other side of the argument. I mean, you know so much, Finn: you could make people really think.'

But he's lost it. He sits in glum silence. We cycle back without talking at all.

Fourteen

'Sit down, for a moment!' Mum says. 'You're always rushing off out somewhere, or coming back from somewhere! We've hardly seen you for days.'

'And? Your point is?'

'Kate!' Dad starts saying, but Mum interrupts him.

'No, David. I'm handling this, thank you very much'.

She turns back to me. 'It would be nice to talk to you for a change. More than a brief good morning or goodbye or goodnight. We'd like to hear about what you've been up to. About your new friends. And we need to make a few rules about you telling us where you're off to, and when you'll be back.'

'I don't see why I should tell you anything.' My words come out more stroppy than I intended.

Dad can't contain himself. 'Good manners cost nothing,' he says. 'Show us a bit of respect, Kate.'

That does it.

'Me? Respect you! When you and Mum are so catastrophically disrespecting our family with your horrible rows and silences! And you tell me nothing!

You must think I'm stupid not to see what's really going on. This pretence of happy families when you are on the verge of splitting up . . . And you, Dad! Total hypocrite; phoning some woman every chance you get to go off to that phone box –'

'Stop! Enough!' Mum spits words through tight lips. She's shaking with rage.

Dad walks away to the window and stands there with his hands in his pockets, fiddling with the coins in them, making the annoying chinking sound that drives both me and Mum mad on a good day.

But Mum's crumpled down on the sofa, her head in her hands, weeping softly.

'You phoned her? How could you, David?' she keeps saying. 'After all we discussed. All your promises that you'd really try, for these few weeks of summer.'

So. I guess that means my hunch was right. There *is* someone. Dad *has* been phoning her.

Even though I've imagined this over and over, as if to prepare myself for the worst, the realisation that I was actually right still comes as a horrible shock.

Dad doesn't deny it, doesn't even try.

The room feels suddenly airless, my chest tight with pain.

Mum is crying, needs me, but I can't go to her, can't offer any comfort. All I can think of is myself. My world crumbling, dissolving to dust.

Dad still has his back to us. He doesn't try to explain or excuse himself. I want to hit him, drum his pathetic back with my fists and make him yell, or cry or say *something*.

Sorry would be good.

'Well. Thanks for a great summer holiday,' I say as sarcastically as I can manage. 'Cheers, Mum and Dad.'

I walk to the front door, open it wide, bang it shut so hard the whole house shudders.

Fifteen

The ferry must have come in. There's a line of cars and vans coming slowly along the road through the village, bumping over the cattle grid. I run past the shop and the telephone box, the telecom mast and the hotel, out of the village. I turn left up the hill to find the one spot where my mobile gets a fragment of reception.

I try Bonnie first, but she doesn't answer. Hannah next. But she'll be at work: her phone's turned off. Before I know it, I'm calling Sam.

His phone rings and rings. Then it goes to voice-mail. The stupid automatic message. My hands are shaking. I press *exit*.

Molly?

No answer. I send her a text: **phone me? Please. Kx**

I want to sit down but there's nowhere apart from the edge of the road or the grass, and the minute I sit or even walk on a few paces I've lost reception again. I stand there, on that one spot just above the road, hoping and hoping for a text or a call.

The wind's blowing a gale. I notice for the first time that I'm shivering. A camper van with kayaks on the top goes past and someone waves from the window, as if to thank me for letting them go past.

My phone stays silent. I start walking again, eyes stinging with tears. I'm totally alone on a stupid island miles and miles from anyone and no one even cares.

Geese fly low in a V-shape, calling to each other as they fly. Sheep move slowly, cropping the grass and flowers, bleating to the half-grown lambs who are already getting fat. They scatter in all directions as I get closer.

Where can I go?

Not Finn's house. Not when I'm feeling like this. The only other person I know is Isla, but I don't know her well enough yet and in any case, I don't think she'd understand. I could run down to the pier and get on the next ferry . . . it will be leaving in fifteen minutes or so . . . only I've got no money for the long journey home, don't know if there are any trains even . . .

In the end I just keep walking, over to the other side, the way I went once before in pouring rain.

Today it's dry, at least. This side of the island is more sheltered. The air is warmer, it's quieter out of the wind. The road leads down to the shore, the ruined cottage, a patchwork of small fields bounded by rocks.

The sea's blue, blue, blue all the way to the horizon. The other islands in the archipelago seem to float, green and inviting. All you'd need is a small boat . . .

The usual birds are running in and out of the edge of water, pecking at shrimps and insects or whatever, oblivious to me and my problems. A family of seals plays in the surf. I watch them for ages. A woman with a sheepdog walks the length of the beach and smiles at me as she passes. The world carries on.

I pull out my notebook from my bag and open it. I read through all the pages I've written. It makes me feel more substantial, somehow. I do exist. I am me. This is the story of my heart.

But today, my heart is breaking.

I sit at the edge of the beach until it's beginning to get dark. I watch the way the light changes, the pattern of the sun on the sea, the shadows lengthening. The sound of the birds gets stronger as the daylight fades: they call to each other as they fly home to roost. More geese fly over; two swans and a noisy party of black and white ducks bob along on the sea. Swallows swoop for flies. The little wading birds at the water's edge keep peeping the whole time as if they are doing a running commentary. It seems I've disappeared into the background, invisible to this world of birds and seals and insects because I keep almost completely still. I'm cold to the bone, but I don't feel hungry, don't feel anything much any more.

As the sun gets lower, the moon rises, clear and silver and newly minted, a sliver of light. I think of that first night and the full moon framed in the skylight window

– how it seemed to signal something exciting, the beginning of something new.

A great stillness seems to spread over the water, over the sand, as the darkness covers the island. Stars begin to appear. The sea roars from a distance, but close up the sound of the waves is gentle and muted. The calm spreads right over me too, sitting under a blanket of stars.

Even as late as it is, there is still light in the western sky. Further north, it will be light almost all night. I can imagine that, sitting here.

There is nothing I can do about Mum and Dad now.

It's happened, the worst thing.

And I'm still here, and the world's still here, turning slowly, spinning through space: Sam's glowing blue dot in the black wilderness.

Sixteen

When I finally creep back into the house, I find Mum alone on the sofa, sitting in the dark room. She's not angry with me. She holds out her arms, and I sit beside her, and she holds me close and tight and weeps into my hair. 'I'm sorry, I am so, so sorry,' she says over and over. 'It's not what I wanted for you.'

I don't cry. I rest my head against her warm shoulder. It's soft, comfortable: I could close my eyes and sleep for a hundred years.

'Where's Dad?' I ask her.

'Sleeping,' she says. 'He's exhausted. It's not easy for him either, you know. One day you might begin to understand.'

'Can you tell me?' I ask. 'Can you explain what happened, what went wrong?'

She stiffens slightly. She sighs heavily. 'It's very hard to say, exactly. It's happened over such a long time, so many years. And we still love each other, always will, underneath all the horrible stuff . . .'

It doesn't make sense to me. How can she say that?

'And it's all come to a head, because he's met this . . . this person, but she isn't the real reason for us going our separate ways. Not really.'

'What is, then?' I ask.

Mum sighs. 'The differences between us. The lost sense of a common purpose . . . the way we stopped talking, really talking I mean. The way we both gave up on the other, stopped wanting the very best for each other . . .'

She talks in a sad, loving way about Dad's isolation, his lost sense of self. How can it be too late, when she can talk about him like this?

'And along comes someone who offers a fresh start,' she says. 'A chance to begin anew, without any of the past hurt or the *baggage* that's inevitable in a long relationship. Like being offered a lifeline, a chance to be different. I can see how irresistible it might be.'

She doesn't sound angry now. Just sad and resigned. It's almost unbearable.

'Who is she?' I ask.

'Someone at work,' Mum says. 'Younger than him. Pretty, I suppose, in an insipid sort of way. Definitely *unencumbered*.'

'What does that mean?' I say.

'Well, free. Single, and no children.'

Me, Bonnie and Hannah. *Encumbrances*.

It's an odd word for Mum to use.

'What will happen now?'

'We'll go back home at the end of the holiday as planned. I guess we'll have to sell the house. I'll buy something new, for us to live in. Me and you, I mean.

Hannah and Bonnie too when they want to stay. You can see Dad whenever you want. I suppose he'll move in with the woman.'

She won't say her name.

'It hurts too much,' Mum says. 'It's horrible, all of it. For us all. But please try not to worry too much, Kate darling. It will be all right, in time.'

'No, it won't,' I say. 'Nothing can ever be all right ever again.' I disentangle myself from Mum's arms.

I walk slowly up the stairs. The room is moonlit, waiting for me. I lie in the silvery light, tears trickling down my face, feeling my heart turn to stone.

Seventeen

I wake late: Mum and Dad are already up. I can hear their voices, calm and normal, as they potter around downstairs together. For a second I let myself imagine we've slipped back in time: everything's fine, we're a normal happy family. But I can't pretend for long.

I get up anyway and go down for breakfast with them: I'm going to make a real effort today. For Mum's sake.

Dad's cooking bacon, Mum's clearing the table of books and papers so they can sit down properly. She looks pale, but fine. She's washed her hair, she's wearing her favourite blue skirt.

She smiles at me. 'Want to sit down for breakfast with us?'

I nod.

'Bacon? Toast?' Dad asks. 'Coffee's nearly ready.'

'Toast, please,' I say. I watch him slice the loaf, put it in the toaster, pour milk into a pan to warm for Mum, the way she likes it.

It's as if yesterday never happened.

That's what I think at first, watching Mum and Dad talk about plans for the day, do that domestic dance round the kitchen – the way people who have known each other for years move around a small room together, close but not touching. And then I work out it's *because* of what happened yesterday that it's like this now: the air cleared, nothing secret now, the truth laid bare.

I try to imagine what happened after I left the house, yesterday. Did they talk properly and truthfully at last? Is it a relief, now it's all out in the open?

Even so, this . . . this strange calm, the ordinary conversation . . . it's weird.

I don't know how to *be*. Like I can't rant and stomp and fight if they are being sweet and reasonable and nice to each other . . .

But there's so much I haven't said, yet.

So many questions.

Dad sits down. He pours coffee for everyone, hands Mum the jug of hot milk.

'Do Bonnie and Hannah know?' I blurt out. 'Have you told them?'

'Not yet,' Dad says. 'We thought we should talk to them face to face, not over the phone. And there's no hurry. I mean, nothing is going to change immediately.'

'We will try and make things as easy and harmonious as possible for you and Bonnie and Hannah,' Mum says. 'We both still love you, the same as always. We still love each other, actually. Despite how it looks –'

125

'Why are you splitting up, then? It doesn't make any sense.'

Mum is unnaturally calm. 'I know. It's very hard to understand.' She looks at Dad, as if she wants him to help her explain.

He puts down his mug of coffee, clears his throat. 'I know it's hard, Kate. But these things happen. Relationships change over time. It's inevitable. People change. Want different things. Your mother and I . . . well, we will always be your parents, nothing can change that, and we'll go on sharing that, even if we're not actually living together. We both want the best for you and Hannah and Bonnie. Living in the middle of conflict and tension isn't good for anyone, especially you, we both know that. And this way, at least things can settle down and be a bit calmer. A fresh start all round. You girls will be fine.' He walks over to the window, stands there with his back to us, staring out.

It's so quiet in the room I can hear the sea outside. My heart's pounding. I don't know if I am simply furious or just deeply, horribly sad. Both, probably. In my head I count slowly to a hundred, and another hundred. I take deep breaths.

Dad starts speaking again. 'I'm sorry,' he says. 'One day I hope you will understand. When you fall in love, perhaps, for the first time –' He says something about the woman, but I put my hands over my ears.

'I don't want to hear anything about her, ever,' I say. 'I think what you have done to Mum, and all of us, is terrible. How can you possibly think anyone in the whole world is more lovely than Mum? You don't know what *love* means.'

'Kate!' Mum says. Her hands are white, clenched fists.

'It's all right,' Dad says. 'I understand you're angry.'

'You understand NOTHING!' I yell. I push the table back, run upstairs into my room.

I fling myself on to the bed.

I can hear them moving around downstairs. Mum's sobbing. Dad's voice, muffled. I lie on the bed, staring up at the squares of blue cloudless sky, try to wipe my mind clean so I don't have to think about anything.

I hear the sounds of someone washing up the breakfast dishes. The click of the radio being turned on. Voices. A door opens and bangs shut again. Silence.

I turn my face into the pillow.

I don't know how long I lie there. I must have gone back to sleep at some point. When I wake up, I assume they've both gone out, but eventually I hear feet padding up the stairs and Dad comes into my room.

He sits down on the end of the bed.

I keep my face pressed into the pillow. I won't look at him.

'I never wanted to hurt you,' Dad says. 'I never meant things to turn out like this. I really didn't.'

'Why can't you try again?' I ask. 'You and Mum.'

Dad doesn't speak.

When I turn over to look at him, he's got tears running down his face. I don't think I've ever seen him cry before. It makes me start crying all over again.

127

He takes my hand in his. He holds it tight.

'It's too late for Mum and me,' he says. 'But I'll never stop loving you, Kate. You know that, don't you?'

I nod. I do, deep down.

Something's different, after that. A weird kind of equilibrium and peacefulness comes over the three of us. We all make a huge effort to be gentle with each other, and although it's incredibly hard at first, it gets easier as the day goes on. It's as if now everything is out in the open, we can all relax a little.

I go with them for a walk. We take books to read at the beach and buy picnic things from the shop. Dad brings the binoculars and I try to learn some of the names of the birds he points out. *Tern. Sanderling. Curlew . . .*

The wind has dropped. Tomorrow is Saturday, Tim's birthday. The weather is perfect.

'Can I go to a beach party tomorrow evening with Finn and his brothers and friends?' I ask. 'They're taking tents so we can stay overnight.'

'Does it involve boats?' Dad asks. 'Or cars?'

'No.'

Dad looks at Mum. 'What do you reckon?'

'It sounds like a lovely thing to do. A perfect way to spend a midsummer night. Of course Kate should go.'

'But no drinking alcohol,' Dad says. 'They're much older than you, remember. You don't have to join in with everything they're getting up to.'

Mum smiles sadly. 'Honestly, David!' she says.

'Listen to yourself. Try remembering what it's like being fifteen. You were, once!'

'That's the trouble,' Dad says. 'I remember it only too well!'

Mum and I paddle in the sea: later, I actually swim. It's freezing, of course, like last time, but it's easier to swim when the waves aren't breaking and crashing. It's almost completely calm.

I let myself float on my back for a moment: the sun's warm on my face, all I can see is blue: blue water, spangled with sunlight; blue sky arching above.

Mum watches me from the water's edge.

'Come in!' I call to her.

She shakes her head. She walks slowly away along the beach, paddling in the shallow water. She walks further and further away until she's just a dark, solitary figure silhouetted against the light.

Dad's watching her too. But he stays put, his book open beside him on the picnic rug.

I stay in as long as I can bear to. But I'm shivering, my hands blue with cold, feet numb. I stumble out of the water; Dad comes to meet me with my towel.

'Thanks, Dad.' I wrap myself in the towel, walk back up the beach with him. He picks up his book, carries on reading.

Mum's just a dot in the distance now.

'You're always reading,' I say to Dad. 'Why don't you ever write things yourself?'

He looks up from his book. 'I write all the time. It's part of my job, Kate.'

'I don't mean reports and lesson plans; I mean your own, creative things, like poems, or stories. Or songs even, like you used to do.'

'Do you remember that? Me writing songs?'

'Mum told me. She said you used to take photographs too.'

'I wasn't much good,' Dad says. 'I did it for myself really.'

'Exactly! For yourself, for fun. Isn't that the point?'

He laughs suddenly. 'Out of the mouths of babes and sucklings . . .' He notices my blank face. 'Don't you know that expression? About the wisdom of the young.'

'Well, then.'

Mum and Dad decide to go back via the local pottery; I turn off towards the Manse. I'm half expecting them all to be out, but no, the cars and jeep are parked outside and I find Joy, Alex and Tim at the garden table drinking tea.

'I came to find out about the party,' I say.

'I'll collect you about seven,' Tim says. 'Didn't you find the note I left at your house?'

'No,' I say, blushing. 'I've been out all day with my parents. Thanks.'

'Is everything all right?' Joy asks. 'Do you want some tea? Shall I go and find Finn for you?'

'No, thank you,' I say quickly. 'I need to get back.'

'You must bring your parents round for tea sometime,' Joy says. 'We'd love to meet them, wouldn't we, Alex?'

'Of course,' he says. 'I understand your dad's a bit of a naturalist himself.'

'Fiona mentioned it,' Joy explains. 'Nothing stays secret for long on an island like this!' She smiles.

What else have they heard?

'I can cycle over here tomorrow if that makes things easier,' I say. 'I've got the bike now. Finn lent it to me.'

'OK. That's a good idea. Then you and Finn can make your own way to the beach. But if there's anything heavy you want to bring, we can shove it in the back of the jeep easy enough.'

'Just bring yourself!' Tim says. 'That's all that's needed.'

'And some warm clothes!' Joy smiles. 'It'll get chilly at night, even with a fire. We'll bundle a whole load of sleeping bags into the jeep, just in case.'

I walk back to the village. A boat trip's about to leave: a crowd of people are standing at the end of the old pier waiting to go on board. There's a family with three little girls in straw sunhats. I swallow hard. That's how we must have looked once: a happy family on holiday together.

Someone's in the red phone box. For a second I'm thinking *Dad* and then I see it's not: some man about the same age, but wearing a suit. Weird. He'll be someone to do with the wind farm project, I guess. Someone official. Poor Finn, I think. Wanting so much to stop things changing. And you just can't sometimes.

*   *   *

Mum looks up as I go inside the house. 'Everything OK?'

I nod. 'How was the pottery?'

'Interesting. Lots of lovely things. See what we got?' She shows me two coffee cups.

Blue, gold.

A hare, running.

They're beautiful.

'Dad bought them for me,' she says.

He's watching birds through the binoculars, as usual. But there's a notebook open beside him on the windowsill, a pen beside it; something scribbled in black ink.

Something shifts inside me, seeing that: almost a click, like a key turning in a lock. Hard to say what it means: just the tiniest bubble of hope.

At bedtime, I lie awake under the open window, watching the stars. This time tomorrow, I'll be out all night, on a beach. Anything might happen. Anything at all.

Because nothing stands still.

Nothing.

Not people, or feelings, or the world itself, turning, turning.

Eighteen

Finn is waiting for me at the Manse: I'm late. The others have already left.

'Sorry,' I say. 'It took longer than I thought by bike.'

'I'm not surprised, with all that on the back! What on earth have you brought?'

'Just a cake, and a bottle, and extra clothes in case it's cold.'

'How sensible you are,' he says, in a way which makes me wish I wasn't.

'I'm thirsty already,' I say. 'Can I have a glass of water before we set off?'

Joy's in the kitchen. She runs the tap for me so the water's dead cold and fills the glass.

'Thanks,' I say.

Suddenly the Manse kitchen seems so cosy and familiar and warm I wish I could stay longer. A bit of me longs to tell Joy what's happened to me and Mum and Dad. I just know she'd be kind and put her arms round me and hold me for a moment, make me feel safe.

But Joy's busy. She waves us off. 'Have a lovely night. It's absolutely perfect: almost balmy. You'll see the sun set, and the stars come out, and before you know it, it'll be dawn.'

'Is it far?' I ask Finn.

'Five miles or so,' he says.

We push up the hill towards the road. Finn seems distracted.

'Have you had a nice day?' I ask him. 'Did you do lots of birthday things for Tim?'

'No,' he says. 'He was out most of the day, getting stuff ready for his party. He's Piers's and Jamie's friend, not mine, in any case.'

We plod on up the hill.

'I went back to that exhibition,' he says.

'And?'

'And nothing.' He looks at me. 'Why don't you give me that bag? It'll make your bike easier to push.'

'OK. If you're sure. Thanks, Finn,' I say.

He waits while I untie the bag and hand it over. I can't work out what's the matter with him. Is it the wind farm stuff, or something to do with Tim, or is it me?

He seems happier as soon as we get to the road and can actually cycle. The road flattens and straightens; we bowl along at a good speed, the wind behind us. The sky is deep blue, fading to turquoise and green. The road is empty; the fields either side are gold with ripe barley; all I can hear is the swish of the bike wheels, the occasional baaing of sheep, the wind in the grass. It's as if we are cycling to the end of the earth. What was that word? *Finisterre* . . .

'OK,' Finn says, slowing down. 'The beach is just over there. We can go the long way round by the road, or take a short cut over the grass. Short cut?'

I nod.

We get off and push the bikes over the machair and down a steep bank of dunes. There's no proper path. The bike wheels stick in the sand; the sharp edges of marram grass scratch my bare legs as we push our way through. Should've worn jeans, like I usually do, but Isla always wears skirts, and this once I thought I would. It is a party, after all . . .

'Oh, wow! It's beautiful!' I say, as we come over the top of the dunes to the other side. It's another amazing beach, with gleaming white sand: crushed shell, and turquoise sea. I can see people swimming, way out.

Tim's set up camp further along the sand: the jeep's parked up on a strip of grass where the track comes down to the beach from the road. We push the bikes along the beach in that direction. It's hard work, through soft sand.

Piers and Jamie are building a fire at the top of the beach next to an outcrop of striped rock. Bags and boxes are piled up nearby.

Tim waves as we get closer.

I wave back. 'Happy Birthday!' I call.

Isla's already here, looking amazing in a pale green

135

dress, her hair loose down her back. She's sitting next to Tim, opening bottles of beer and handing them round. She passes a bottle to Finn.

'Kate?' She offers me one but I shake my head. She laughs. 'I forgot; you're only fifteen.'

'It's not that,' I say. 'I don't like beer, that's all.'

'Well, there's plenty of other stuff.' She waves her arm towards the boxes stacked on the rocks. 'Help yourself.'

The fire starts to crackle and spit and send up sparks. The damp bits of wood sizzle and steam.

Thea and Clara run up the beach, dripping from their swim, and dash off again, playing tag and larking about, laughing. Piers and Jamie watch them.

Tim does too. He grins at Isla. 'Surprised you didn't swim. You usually do.'

'I am full of surprises.' She's blatantly flirting with him. 'There's plenty of time for swimming, in any case.'

She looks at me. 'How about it, Kate? Fancy a dip later under the stars?'

I smile but don't answer. I don't know what to say. I haven't brought swimming things. I know *she* wouldn't let that be a problem. It's probably what they all do, skinny-dipping under the stars . . .

Finn's downed his beer already. He picks at a loaf of bread and breaks off a lump of cheese to go with it. There's a kind of tension running in the air; like electricity, fizzing round Tim, Isla, Finn . . .

'The sea's not that cold this evening,' Thea says, as she comes back up the beach to get her towel. 'Hello,

Kate.' She changes into jeans and a white shirt; wrings out her dripping hair and sits with her back to the fire to dry it.

Tim pours her a glass of wine.

The tide's a long way out. The sand stretches as far as you can see, white and pure, hardly touched except where the girls ran and danced after their swim and left their spiralling trail of footprints.

I'm watching everything, but not quite part of it. Don't feel as if I belong here really. Not just because I'm younger . . . it's that they all know each other so well. And I'm still thinking about Mum and Dad. Our family, broken. I can't stop.

I slip off my shoes, sit with feet buried in the dry sand at the top of the beach, feel it trickle through my toes. The geese are calling. I watch them fly over, and the feeling washes over me again: a yearning sadness for what I've lost, can't have, ever again . . .

I pull myself back. *Stop it! It doesn't change anything. And I'm here at a party, for God's sake. Tim's birthday. Be here,* I tell myself firmly. *Now. In the moment.*

I remember the cake. I go to find the plastic box in my bag, hand it to Tim. 'For you,' I say.

He takes off the lid. 'Hey, a proper birthday cake, with candles and icing! You sweetheart! Thank you, Kate.' He kisses the top of my head briefly.

'It's only small,' I say.

'That's perfect, because Joy made us a cake too. Not as pretty as yours though.'

He passes the box round for everyone to admire.

'Mmm. Chocolate,' Piers says. 'My favourite.'

'Let's save it for pudding,' Thea says. 'We should definitely wait for it to be dark before you light the candles.'

A crowd of people arrive, other friends of Tim's, people he's got to know on the island over the years he's been visiting the Manse. They are polite enough, but they don't take much notice of me. I'm much younger than everyone else except Finn and Isla.

The sun's low in the sky, casting long shadows. The sky is turning pink and gold in the west. More birds fly over, whole flocks of them. Finn watches them. I tell him the ones I know now. Oystercatchers, terns, and sand-pipers. Black-backed gulls. Greylag geese. I'm getting better. I know lots more than I did just two weeks ago.

I'm starving: it must be at least nine and the only thing I've eaten all day is toast and the scrapings from the cake mixture. I help myself to bread and cheese.

Finn notices. 'We could start cooking,' he says. 'The fire's easily hot enough now. Want to help?'

It's nice having something to do. Thea takes over after a while, and organises us. Tim gets steaks and home-made burgers out of a cool box and starts cook-ing them on a metal grill balanced on stones over the white hot heart of the fire. Isla helps him. They laugh, look at each other; he keeps touching her arm.

The smell of sizzling meat fills the air. Finn and I get the bowls of salads out of the bags, posh crisps, chutneys and sauces. I arrange slivers of smoked salmon on a plate; slice a lemon into pale yellow circles to decorate it.

Tim opens bottles of champagne: everyone has a glass, including me. And it's a proper glass, not a plastic one. It's like being in a film: I imagine describing it all to Molly. Piers holds up his glass for a toast. 'Happy Birthday, Tim.' We all join in.

Everyone but me has a second glass of champagne.

Tim makes a slightly drunken speech about the importance of friends. While we're all still eating, Jamie sets up speakers for music. Some people begin to dance on the sand. A small group of us watch for the moment when the sun actually sinks beneath the horizon.

'Wait for the green flash,' Finn says, but it never comes. Instead, the sun bleeds liquid gold into the sea and slips down into the dark.

'Try some of this,' Tim says. 'Just a little, because of your tender age. It's not a party without a wee dram.' He pours some amber-coloured drink into my empty glass and I drink it in tiny sips, even though it burns my throat.

'Ten-year-old single malt,' Finn tells me, 'from Islay. The island, not the girl.'

'We should build up the fire again,' Thea says. 'The air's much colder now the sun's gone.'

Jamie appoints himself chief fire-tender. He adds more wood: huge heavy timbers from a broken boat, or a rotten pier or something. He builds it up, a pyramid taller than himself.

'Enough!' Clara pulls at Jamie's sleeve. 'Careful! You're like a man possessed!'

Flames stalk up the salt-crusted edges, lick and flare. Every time he throws on more wood, showers of glowing red sparks fly skywards. He grins. 'There! Isn't it wonderful?'

Some of the guests leave. 'Thanks, Tim, lovely party! Goodbye!' Their voices call like birds through the dusk. They walk back up the track to the road.

For a while the music plays on, people dance. The mood changes as darkness covers the beach. The sea sounds louder, roaring, as the tide begins to come back in. The edges of everything seem blurred and fuzzy. Where sky meets sea, or sea meets land, or the boundaries between one person and another. I hold my arm at full stretch and look at my hand: even my own body is merging into the landscape.

'Now is a good time to swim,' Isla says, 'with the tide coming in over the sun-warmed sand.' She moves further away, into the dark. She strips off her clothes. I can just make out her pale limbs as she runs down to the sea. 'Come on!' she calls.

Finn starts pulling his jumper over his head, unzipping his jeans, stepping out of them.

'Be careful,' Thea warns him. 'Swimming and alcohol are not a good mix . . .'

He's not listening. He's already following Isla down to the sea.

Thea looks at Piers.

'All right,' he says, as if she's asked him a question. 'I'll go.' He gets up and walks slowly down the beach after them.

Jamie laughs. 'He's the good brother,' he says.

Thea frowns. 'The sea can be dangerous,' she says.

Out of the corner of my eye I notice Tim, standing up, staring towards the sea. He starts walking, not seawards but towards the jeep. He opens the door, gets in.

'Piers left the keys in,' Thea says.

Jamie shrugs. 'Oh, well.'

The engine starts up. Next minute, Tim's driving the jeep on to the sand, revving the engine as the wheels get clogged, then getting up speed. He drives in wide, crazy circles over the beach: I can't see properly, just hear the engine, see the grey shape appearing and disappearing. My heart thuds against my ribcage. *No. Not this. Not again . . .*

Jamie jumps up; he runs after the jeep, yelling and whooping with excitement. Not to stop him, but to climb in too.

'So stupid!' Thea says.

The jeep comes back up the beach towards us: Tim brakes just in time, before he hits a line of low rocks.

Laughter. Shouts of glee. They open the doors, and haul Clara in too. Tim switches on the lights: the beams are blinding. Thea puts her hand over her eyes.

'Kate? You coming for a spin?' Tim calls.

I shake my head. 'I'm looking after the fire,' I say, heart racing.

The jeep veers off again, much too fast, wheels spinning in the sand.

'Ridiculous!' Thea says again. 'Dangerous and foolish!' She looks at me. 'I'm glad you have more sense, Kate. Not drunk, like they all are.'

'Just scared,' I tell her.

I nearly tell her about Sam, and me, and a car journey that could have ended everything for ever. But I stop. It's a party, I tell myself. Stop being like this. It's a huge beach. There are no other cars. It's all fine . . .

The two of us sit, knees hunched up, staring into the darkness, listening to the cries and shouts blown over the beach, the sound of the engine, harsh and unnatural. Tyres, brakes squealing. Someone presses the horn and the sound of it, on and on, makes my heart pound and my palms sweat.

'It isn't funny.' Thea peers into the dark. 'And where are Piers and Finn and Isla? They've been ages.' She stands up again.

I get up to stand next to her.

'It's OK,' I say. 'I can see Piers, I think: there, right down near the sea.'

As we stare into the dark, the jeep judders into view again, coming along the beach very fast, heading for the sea this time.

Tim swerves it in and out of the shallow water at the edge, laughing and shouting, as if he's having the best fun ever.

'For heaven's sake!' Thea says. 'Has he gone totally crazy?'

He's changed utterly from the sensible grown-up Tim I know into someone quite different. I'm full of fear now, and fury too . . .

'He's lost it completely!' Thea says. 'He shouldn't be driving at all in that state. It's madness. And why aren't the others stopping him? Instead they're all egging him on. It's totally irresponsible of them.'

'What –!'

The jeep's stopped, still in the water; there's a second of ominous silence. Then laughter, and shouting. 'It's stuck!'

'Out everybody! All push!'

The wheels are wedged into the wet sand. The incoming waves rush in, foaming against the wheels.

Piers runs over to help. 'What the f– !'

Tim doesn't seem to have any sense of danger or responsibility. The sea's coming in. It's not even his car. No one has a rope or anything to tow it out of the water. And he and Jamie and Clara are still laughing so much they haven't the strength to push properly . . .

Someone yells out.

Thea rolls up her jeans and runs down to the sea.

But I'm paralysed, unable to move. Memories are flooding in – all the details of that night that I've been trying so hard to forget. Sam exhilarated by the speed of the car, driving faster and faster; the look on his face as a car pulls out in front of us . . . him overtaking it. Then blinding lights and the horrible, long squeal of car tyres on wet tarmac . . . Glass breaking. Metal, thumping and crashing over the edge of the road . . . Someone calling out . . .

My heart's hammering in my chest so hard I can hardly breathe . . . I'm shaking, crouched and terrified in the dark, as if it's going to happen all over again.

No.

I make a huge effort to steady myself.

You're OK, I tell myself. *That's all over and done with. You survived. You're safe now. Sitting on a beach* . . .

Breathe, deeply.

I begin to hear voices again: the real voices of Tim and the others. Here, and now.

'Run, get your phone and call someone,' Tim shouts. 'Anybody who lives nearby who'd have a rope and a four-wheel drive . . .'

'There's no signal, you idiot!' Piers shouts back.

Isla's already sprinting up the beach, Finn close behind her. They pull on their clothes, take their bikes, disappear up the track.

They'll find someone to help.

It will be all right.

Gradually I calm down.

I hug my knees, rock myself in the dark.

Nineteen

Thea's voice. 'The tide's running in fast. It's getting too deep to stand. Why aren't Isla and Finn back with some help?'

A car comes slowly along the road behind the dunes. Its headlights reflect off the pale grass, light up the sky. But the car carries on round the sweep of the bay. The lights fade into the distance.

The sea's crashing on to the rocks at the edge of the beach, sending up plumes of spray. It sounds louder than ever.

'OK,' Tim says. His voice carries clearly across the sand. He sounds totally sober now: serious and focused. 'One final lift and push, to see whether we can release the wheels.'

'It's shifting a bit,' Thea shouts. 'The water is actually lifting the jeep.'

I watch it all as if through a distant lens, as if I'm not actually on the beach with them at all, as if I'm watching a scene in some film unfolding before me.

No one notices that I'm not helping. Everyone's attention is on getting the jeep out of the sea.

They finally manage to drag it on to the wet sand at the edge of the water.

Tim tries to turn the engine. Absolutely nothing happens, of course. Not a sound or a flicker of life.

'How the hell am I going to explain this to your parents?' Tim says to Piers.

'A bit late to be wondering about that.'

Everyone else has gone totally quiet.

'How high will the tide come up?' Thea asks.

'Higher than this,' Piers says. 'So we need to move the jeep further up the beach somehow.'

'We should get warmed up first,' Thea says. 'I'm totally freezing, we all are. We've got a bit of time, haven't we? Enough so we can change out of wet clothes.'

Someone piles more wood on the fire. Piers and Jamie find the camping stove that Joy stashed in one of the boxes for an emergency and Piers sets up a pan of water for hot drinks. Thea finds blankets too. She passes one to me. 'Are you OK, Kate?'

I nod. I'm still shivering.

'We should put up the tent,' Clara says.

'No need,' Jamie says. 'It's not going to rain. The sky is clear.'

I look up. For the first time for hours, it seems.

'Someone's coming at last!' Tim says. 'See?'

Headlights arc across the sky, lighting up the dune-grass next to the beach road. The car comes nearer. It slows, turns off the road and bumps down the track to the beach. Another jeep.

Tim walks over to greet Isla and Finn as they jump out.

He shakes hands with the driver.

'This is Rob,' Isla says. 'He works with my dad sometimes.'

The man looks amused, rather than angry. 'Been having fun and games, I hear,' he says.

Tim doesn't speak.

'Well, you got her out of the sea,' Rob says. 'That's the hard work done. Pretty impressive. I can tow her further up the beach for you.'

'Thanks,' Piers says.

'Then we'd best wait till the morning, to let her dry out a bit before we see the damage. But your luck's in; I've a mate who's a mechanic. He'll sort you out, if anyone can.'

Tim looks terrible now he's realised the full extent of what he's done. Everyone's thinking about Alex and Joy.

Piers helps tie the rope and Tim climbs in to steer as Rob tows the jeep up the sand. It only takes a minute.

Thea stirs chocolate powder into the boiling water, and pours it into cups. Jamie produces another bottle of whisky. 'A shot of this will warm us up.'

'Not for me, thanks all the same,' Rob says. 'Seeing as I'm driving.' He laughs, but Tim looks mortified.

'You chose the right night for a bit of a party,' Rob says. 'Not often we get such a clear one as this.'

'It's Tim's birthday,' Thea explains. 'We should cut the cakes,' she says. 'We forgot all about them earlier.'

'I'll leave you to it,' Rob says. 'It's late. I need to be up early in the morning. I'll tell my mate to call round sometime tomorrow, sort you out.'

No one knows quite what to say to Tim. He's very quiet.

Isla goes to sit next to him after a while. Finn's watching every move she makes.

'Mackie's a good mechanic,' she says. 'He'll have all the spare parts at the garage. He'll know what to do.'

Tim carries on sitting with his head bowed. He doesn't even look at her.

'OK. Cake.' Thea says brightly. 'And candles for you, Tim.'

'Is it still Tim's birthday?' Clara asks. 'Isn't it way after midnight?'

'I suppose,' Thea says. 'But we're still doing the candles. And singing.'

'Kate, you light them, seeing as you made the cake.' Piers chucks a box of matches in my direction.

Hearing my own name makes me jump. I'd somehow thought I'd become totally invisible. No one asks me why I didn't help, or what I've been doing all this time.

My hands are still shaking. I find it hard to light all the little candles at the same time: they keep going out.

'Everyone get closer,' Thea says. 'Make a human windbreak.'

Eventually I manage to light all twenty-three

148

candles, and they stay alight for a few seconds. Long enough, anyway.

'Ahhh. Perfect,' Isla says. 'It's really pretty, Kate.'

Tim blows the candles out and everyone sings. Except me; I still don't trust my voice to come out right.

Everyone's getting sleepy. After a while, Jamie and Piers unpack the sleeping bags and blankets. People arrange themselves around the fire. The wood is glowing, red hot, but the flames have died down now.

'I'll keep it going all night,' Jamie promises.

We lie on our backs, staring at the amazing sky: a blanket pinned with a million stars. The Milky Way is a bright silver band.

'This is the best month for shooting stars,' Finn says. 'August, there are always loads. The Perseid meteor shower . . .'

He shifts his sleeping bag closer to mine. 'You OK, Kate?' he whispers.

I nod. I swallow hard. The night sky is so beautiful, and my heart so full, but still I cannot speak.

He reaches out for my hand and squeezes it tight, and lets it go.

'You'll be fine,' he says, as if he's known all along that something is wrong. 'Keep watching for falling stars.'

But I have to close my eyes tight, to stop the tears from coming.

When I open them next and look round, I see that Isla has moved her sleeping bag closer to Tim. They're lying close enough to be almost touching. Perhaps they are: I can't tell from here, in the dark.

Finn's still gazing at the stars.

The fire shifts and stirs. Embers fall to white ash. I snuggle deeper into the sleeping bag.

Thea and Piers are talking quietly to each other, their murmuring voices merging with the sound of the sea. The sound is comforting.

I'm warm at last, tired, almost asleep . . .

'What's that?'

'What?'

Voices: Tim's, and Isla's, muffled and sleepy. For a second, I am confused. I blink in the darkness, slowly coming to. The fire's burned so low for a second I think it's gone out. Tim stirs it with a stick, adds a log. White ash falls and glows.

Isla sits up. 'Oh my God! Look, Tim.'

A shooting star?

But it's something even more amazing. Not stars, or a full moon, or anything I have ever seen before except in pictures.

The sky is rippling with a weird kind of light. Like a billowing curtain, shifting through shades of green, and silver, and white. A huge veil, moving and swaying in the northern sky.

'What is it? What's happening?' Jamie and Piers are awake too now, sitting up, stumbling out of their sleeping bags to get a better view. 'Sunrise? Already?'

'It's the Northern Lights,' Isla says. 'How extraordinary.'

Everyone's wide awake now.

The light flows like water, like wind made visible,

like nothing I have ever seen before. It fades, and brightens, and for a second disappears, then comes back, wild and rippling and dancing.

'Oh my God!' Clara says.

'Awesome.'

'I can't believe it!'

Is it possible? Are we really looking at the Northern Lights, here, on a beach in the Hebrides, in the middle of an August night?

Isla says that it is perfectly possible. That it happens once every eleven years or so. 'It's to do with solar energy or something.'

'The aurora borealis,' Tim says.

The air's alive and breathing: a sound like hissing, or whispering, or the crackling of a fire . . .

Can you really *hear* light?

'The music of the heavens,' Thea says. 'That's astonishing!'

'The Finnish word for the aurora means *fox fires*,' Finn whispers. 'The Sami people believe it's caused by a fox running across the frozen fields of the north, its tail sweeping the snow and sending up light.

'And in Inuit legend, the lights are the torches of skydweller spirits, guiding the feet of new arrivals – spirits of the newly dead. The whistling noise is the voices of the spirits trying to communicate with the people of the earth. You're supposed to answer in whispers.'

Clara giggles.

'I've seen it once before,' Isla says, 'when I was five or six. And my dad remembers being carried from his bed as a child, out into the field, to watch the Northern Lights.'

We watch and listen in silence for a long time.

The lights fade, and disappear completely.

We wait.

Just an ordinary night sky now.

Though there is nothing *ordinary* about it. So many stars, planets. A satellite, tracking round. More stars. The vast and beautiful universe.

It comes to me, like a revelation: Sam's photo.

The miracle of it.

That's what he wanted me to see.

A night bird calls. Someone murmurs in their sleep.

Already, there's light in the eastern sky. It won't be long till dawn.

Twenty

In the early morning sunlight, everything shines. Silver light glints off the sea, reflects in the pools of water on the ridged sand. The tide has gone down again. I can hear voices: faint laughter. Tim and Isla are swimming together, their heads dark like seals. I watch them swim out side by side and then stop, turn on to their backs to float for a moment, and come together in an embrace. I look away.

I know Finn's awake and has seen them too.

Last night he was happy; he swam with her, went with her to get help. But later, by the fire, and in the night, it was obvious that it's Tim she wants to be with, not him.

Is it always like this? The two who are happy, the unhappy third?

I wriggle out of my sleeping bag. The air is cool. I stoke up the fire with driftwood.

Finn watches me. 'Put on smaller bits of wood to begin with, to get it going,' he says.

'OK.' I don't usually like people telling me how to do things, but he's right, it does work better. Flames lick along the thin strips of wood, the fire begins to rustle and spit as it comes to life.

'Do you want a walk with me, before everyone wakes up?' Finn asks.

'Yes,' I say. 'I'd love that.'

We don't mention the fact that Tim and Isla are already up. I pull on my boots and my thick jumper. Everything else, I'm wearing already: kept it on all night. I stretch out my spine, ease out the stiffness in my shoulders.

We walk across the sand in the opposite direction from Tim and Isla, keeping our backs to them. The jeep stands forlornly in the middle of the beach. We walk past it.

Finn stops. 'Hang on.' He runs back, opens the bonnet and leaves it propped up. 'Let the morning sun and the air dry it all out a bit,' he explains when he catches up.

It's still quiet. The seabirds are only just beginning to stir. Black and white oystercatchers stand in rows on the small island of rock offshore, all facing the same way. 'They look as if they're doing some sort of morning ritual,' I say. 'A salute to the sun.'

'They're warming themselves up,' Finn says.

The birds fly off as we get nearer, and their peep-peeping cry echoes mournfully over the bay.

'Why do they sound so sad?' I ask.

'They don't,' Finn answers. 'Not to me, anyway. Perhaps it's because *you* are sad.'

I don't know what to say to that.

'Talk about it,' Finn says. 'I'm good at listening.'

We walk slowly the whole length of the sandy bay and first I tell him about Mum and Dad, and about what will happen when I go home. 'Dad will move out,' I say, and my eyes are full of tears again.

This is how it is going to be, and I've got to get used to it.

'It's tough when parents mess up,' Finn says. 'And there's nothing you can do about it. It's hard seeing how flawed they are, I guess. When you're a child, you don't really think about your parents making mistakes, getting things wrong, wanting different things for themselves. It's part of growing up, having to face that they're just human, and fallible.'

'But they do their best,' I insist. 'I know they love me. Mum hasn't done anything wrong.'

'No?'

'What do you mean?'

'There are always two sides to a story. Things are not simply right or wrong. One person's fault. They are shades of grey, rather than black and white.'

We stop at the rocks and sit there, staring out to sea. A cormorant is diving for fish, surfacing, going under again. Finn gets the binoculars out of his pocket. 'There's a diving bird out there too,' he says. 'A black-throated diver. *Gavia arctica*. Quite rare. Take a look.' He passes me the binoculars.

It's hard to see in the brightness of the sun. I can make out two birds, dark coloured, one smaller than the other.

155

'Who taught you the names of everything?' I ask.

'My parents, to begin with. Now I teach myself. Look things up. I like knowing the names. It makes me pay particular attention to the detail of each bird, or plant. What makes it special and individual.'

'You're like my dad!' I say.

'Is that a good thing or a bad thing?'

'Neither,' I say. 'It's neutral. A shade of grey, I mean.'

He laughs. 'You learn fast,' he says.

I pass the binoculars back, sit quietly next to him while he watches the water.

'It's very comforting being with you,' I tell Finn. 'You make me feel calm, and steadier, somehow.'

As soon as I've said that out loud, I'm remembering Finn in the exhibition hall at Martinstown. Finn upset and angry, not calm at all. And then I realise that I'm getting to know him, that's all. I'm seeing him as a whole person, beginning to understand him, see his strengths and his weaknesses and accept it all. That's what you have to do to get closer to someone. Not imagine it all, make it up in your head: a fantasy person.

Is that the mistake I made with Sam? Did I make up a person in my head, and it wasn't who he really was at all? Or was it simply that I could see something in him that no one else saw: the real Sam underneath all the other stuff?

'There's this boy,' I start. 'Sam.' I pause. I watch a tiny blue butterfly flit across the rocks. It settles, spreads out its wings in the sun.

Finn looks at me. 'Yes?'

'Can I tell you about him?'

Finn nods. 'If you want to.'

'Sam – I met him at the bus stop – quite random really. He went to the boys' school, not my one. He was older than me. Good-looking. Funny and original and surprising. He was doing A Level sciences: he was really clever. At least, clever about things like physics and geography; mad about the stars and planets and the origins of the universe and all that sort of thing. He could have done anything he wanted. Could have gone out with anyone he wanted, but he chose me.'

Finn frowns slightly. 'Why wouldn't he? You're clever and pretty and interesting too. I don't know why you are so surprised when people like you.'

I let that sink in.

'So? What happened?'

'There was a much darker side to him I didn't see at first. I gradually realised I couldn't tell what he really thought about me. He'd be friendly and lovely one day, and then he wouldn't phone me for ages – I didn't know what was going on. His family was messed up – I mean, I know mine is too, but not like that. His was in a whole different league. There wasn't enough food for the kids to eat even – he ended up living with his nan half the time. I worked it all out gradually. He wouldn't tell me anything. I suppose he wanted to keep it all hidden. Like he was ashamed of it.'

'You're talking about him in the past tense.'

'Am I? Well, it's all over, that's why. The night after he passed his driving test – he borrowed his gran's old car, as a kind of celebration. She didn't even know, I realised afterwards. *Freedom*, he said. *At last we can get out of this dump!*

'To begin with it was fine, until we got out of town. He said he was fed up with going along at thirty. He wanted to see how fast he could go.

'I was terrified. He wouldn't listen to me. I didn't know what to do. It was late by then. There wasn't much traffic luckily. But then this car came out of a side road, and we had to slow right down again and it made him mad. He started swearing and revving the engine, and then he swerved out to overtake, but there was a bend in the road . . . and another car coming – I thought we were going to die.'

'But you didn't. Obviously.'

'No, we didn't die.

'We got past the car in front, just – and the car coming the other way – it had to swerve and we didn't crash head on like I thought we were going to – but that car lost control, and it went off the road – there was a huge crash – breaking glass, the most horrible sound –'

'Hey,' Finn says, 'Kate – you don't have to tell me –'

'But I do, I really want to.' I pull myself together, take a deep breath. 'I screamed at him to stop. I don't think he would have done, if I hadn't screamed so much. He'd have kept on driving. He was silent, and shaking and scared. I said we had to go back and help. I dialled 999 and I think the person in the car

158

behind us must have done that already, because the ambulances came so quickly and the police and everything.'

'Did he die? The bloke in the car that crashed?'

'It was a woman. No, she didn't die. She broke her leg, and hurt her back, and she'll be in hospital for ages.'

'And Sam?'

'They arrested him for dangerous driving. I had to be a witness. It was awful. But I couldn't lie.'

'No. You couldn't. You did the right thing. None of it was your fault, Kate.'

I'm shaking all over again. I stare at the sea, at the waves rolling in, one after another after another.

'And last night, on the beach – that's what was wrong with you? You were remembering all this?'

I nod.

'So, is he in prison? *Sam.*'

'No. He got bail – and he'll probably get a community order in the end – on account of his promising A levels and school reports and messed-up family and things. He's lucky, I suppose.'

Finn doesn't say anything for a while.

'My parents made me promise not to see him again,' I say.

'And you're surprised? Honestly, Kate! They love you and want to look after you, of course!' He looks at me. 'Did you want to see him, after all that?'

'I don't know – yes, sometimes I did. Still do. It's confusing. I didn't stop liking him, even though what he did was awful.'

'More fool you,' Finn says.

'That's a bit harsh,' I say.

'The truth is sometimes.'

I bite my lip, trying to stop myself crying.

Finn shuffles closer; he puts his arm round me for a quick hug. It's all I can do to stop myself leaning on him, putting my head on his shoulder and sobbing my heart out. If he'd given the slightest sign, I would have done. I'm longing for someone to hold me close, to make me feel safe and wanted.

But he doesn't. He takes his arm away; it's the briefest of hugs.

The blue butterfly's still sunning itself on the rock. Its wings are such frail things, like pale blue tissue with veins of brown and flecks of gold along the edge.

'Common Blue, female,' Finn says. 'Variation found on Western Isles.'

'Sam won't be able to go to university,' I say. 'It's such a waste. He's clever enough to study astronomy or astrophysics or whatever he wanted to do; he could have a brilliant career. But his family won't support him. His nan doesn't have any money. He'll have to get work of some kind. And now he'll have a criminal record.'

The butterfly folds it wings: the undersides are pale fawn and brown, not blue at all. It spreads them again, takes off. For a second it alights on Finn's hand: we watch the way it trembles. It flies off again: tiny and perfect and resilient. The pale blue wings merge into blue sky so I can't see it any longer.

'He'll be all right,' Finn says. 'He'll find a way, if he wants it enough. You should forget about him now.'

'It isn't that easy,' I say.

'No. But you have to *decide* to do it.'

I lie back against the sun-warmed rock and close my eyes. It's all very well for him to say that . . .

We stay there a long time without speaking. Finn has his back to me. He's still staring out to sea.

'What about you?' I ask him. 'Have you got a story about some girl?' I hesitate, then come straight out and ask. 'You really like Isla, don't you?'

'Yes,' he says. 'But she has a thing for Tim, as you can see.' There's an edge to his voice. He clearly doesn't want to talk about this with me.

I don't push it.

At the other end of the beach, smoke from the fire spirals up into the clean air. They're probably all up and cooking breakfast by now. I'm suddenly ravenously hungry.

'Shall we go back?' I say.

'You go. I'm going to stay here a bit longer. Might walk over to the next bay. I'll see you later.'

I glance at his face. That closed look: I recognise it because I get like that too, sometimes. I hesitate for a second: I could offer to go with him. But I don't: he so obviously wants to be by himself.

'Fine,' I say. 'Thanks for listening to me.'

He doesn't reply.

I jog slowly back along the sand. I've got better at it, what with all the cycling and walking I've done these last couple of weeks. It's a beautiful morning.

My feet sink slightly into the soft sand; the wind's at my back; the sun is dazzling on the sea.

I'm full of sadness, about Sam, and about my family, but right now, I realise, I wouldn't want to be anywhere but here.

It's a new, surprising thought.

Twenty–one

Isla and Tim are out of the sea and dressed. They're sitting around with everyone else, eating sausage sandwiches. They aren't holding hands or anything obvious, but you can tell there's something going on between them. I can, anyway. *Poor Finn,* I think briefly.

'Help yourself to food,' Piers says with his mouth full. 'Luckily we left you some.'

'We assumed Finn was with you,' Thea says.

'He was.' I pick up a bread roll and spread it thickly with butter. 'But he wanted to walk on further. The next bay or something. And I was starving, so I came back.'

Everyone's a bit tired after last night. No one says much. I finish my sandwich, help put things away. Finn still isn't back. No one takes much notice.

Mid-morning, a Land Rover bumps slowly down the track: Rob's friend the mechanic. He says hello to Isla. He knows her, of course. 'Quite a night you had, I hear!'

Isla introduces him: his name is Mackie. She goes with him and Tim to inspect the jeep engine. The rest of us doze in the sun. The day heats up. Voices drift across the sand.

By lunchtime Mackie's whistling and making jokes and Tim looks a whole lot happier. They come over for a cup of tea.

'Mackie's a total miracle worker,' Tim says. 'The jeep's going to be all right.'

'Happened to have all the spare parts, that's all,' Mackie says. 'Just don't mention it to anyone else, me working today.'

'Sunday,' Isla explains. 'No one's supposed to work on a Sunday. Not even cut peat or go shopping.'

I wrinkle my nose. 'That must be really annoying.'

'It's actually a good idea,' she says, 'if you think about it. Spending a day with your family and friends instead of working. Those relationships are at the heart of an island community: the bonds that tie people and make them care about each other and help each other in difficult times. Without that, the island wouldn't survive.'

It feels as if she's telling me off.

Finn's still not back. No one seems bothered. It's not unusual, I guess. He often disappears off to do his own thing. I listen to Mackie talking: he seems to like having an audience. He's not as old as he first seemed. He's got the leathery face of someone who's outside in all weathers, but it turns out he's only a bit older than Tim. He's a fisherman as well as a mechanic. Everyone on the island has at least two jobs.

'Apart from the incomers with their holiday homes,' he says. 'They don't do much useful; just bellyache about stuff. Like all the fuss about the fish and chip van. The generator keeping the holidaymakers awake at night or some such nonsense. So now we don't have a fish 'n' chip van at all and we're all the losers.' He grins at Isla.

He tells us he's never lived anywhere but here. He went to the local school, he worked with his dad and his uncle at the garage, he learned to fish with his grandad.

'What do you think about the wind farm project?' I ask him.

Isla glances at me, but she doesn't say anything.

'Hah! Politicians!' Mackie says scornfully. 'They cook up these schemes and they've never even set foot in the place. They don't have the foggiest about how their schemes will affect normal people, change a way of life that's been handed down for generations. They muck about with it all from their smart city office on a bit of paper – or a computer screen these days, most likely. Plans and maps and graphs and statistics, and it all looks grand and ticks all the boxes about renewables and green this and energy that and European funding other. And all of it means nothing if you haven't ever lived in a place like this, or been on a boat in a storm, or tried to walk along the road in wind when it's hurricane force.' He laughs. 'Politician bloke came up from Edinburgh in his suit and spent the day on a ferry that couldn't land because of the waves and the wind blowing a southeasterly. He spent eight hours at sea in a storm and he went all the way back again to Edinburgh the next day without ever setting foot on the island! You'd think that would teach him something.'

'Why don't more people speak out against the plans?' Thea asks.

'Island people have a long history of having to accept what's done to them. They'll complain about it enough afterwards, mind you. And some of the more mouthy incomers are against it for their own reasons, which puts normal folk off.'

'You have to think about why people move over here,' Isla says. 'Quite often they're people running away from something. People who aren't so good at getting on with others, they don't understand how a real community works.' She laughs. 'They forget that they bring themselves with them, wherever they run.'

I wonder what Finn would say to that.

Mackie nods. 'And the fact is, nothing stands still. Things do have to change; people have to adapt. But not all change is good. You have to think about each thing on its own merit. Not accept *everything*.'

Isla looks as if she's going to argue, but she doesn't.

Thea and Piers start packing up the sleeping bags and cooking things. The party's properly over. Jamie and Clara decide to have one final swim before they make their way back to the Manse.

'Anyone else coming in? Thea? Kate?' Clara asks.

Thea shakes her head.

'Sea's too cold for me,' I say. 'And I should be going home.'

I get my stuff together, say goodbye.

Tim gives me a big bear hug. 'Thanks for the cake, clever Kate,' he says. 'Thanks for being here, celebrating my birthday.'

'I'll never forget it.'

'Me neither!' Tim laughs. 'Nearly destroyed thousands of pounds worth of jeep.'

'I meant the Northern Lights,' I say. 'And the beautiful beach, and being with everybody . . .'

I wheel the bike the long way, up the track towards the road.

Going home, I said. But it's just a holiday house, Fiona's house. I'm not sure I'll ever really be going home again. I think about what Isla said about running away. The sort of people who want to move to an island to live, rather than the ones born and raised there. You have to ask what they're running *from*, she said. What they are trying to leave behind. Because we take ourselves with us, wherever we go, however far and remote.

One of those random thoughts pops up: *Home is where the heart is*. It's a quotation from something: no idea what.

Maybe some people get born in the wrong place, or at the wrong time, or to the wrong parents. Or they end up marrying the wrong person, or being in the wrong job, and they have to spend a lifetime finding their way back to where they ought to be.

Where the heart is.

I cycle slowly back. Away from the shelter of the dunes the wind is stronger, blowing against me. As I come down the last slope into the village and past the shop, I see Mum outside the house, pegging washing on the line, even though it is a Sunday. The clothes flap and dance: she's finding it hard to keep the pegs on the line the wind's so strong. Her skirt, hair – everything's tugged sideways by the wind. It's comforting and familiar, this little scene: a snapshot of ordinary life.

I smile, she waves. I pedal across the bumpy ground to the gate and get off.

'How was it?' she calls. 'Have a lovely time?'

'Amazing,' I say. I wheel the bike through the gate and lean it against the white wall of the house. 'Guess what? We saw the Northern Lights!'

'No! In summer? You lucky things! I've always wanted to see that. I can't believe we missed it! Tell me about it.' She picks up the empty washing basket and we go inside together.

Mum clicks on the kettle for coffee and brings her two new cups from the draining board over to the table. It feels like a normal day; we could be living here like this together, and it wouldn't be strange at all. A glimmer of all the possibilities ahead comes into my head: all the choices you can make about where to live, and how, and with whom.

'Where's Dad?' I ask.

'Birdwatching, walking,' she says. 'Having some thinking time.'

We sip coffee. I hold the cup up in both hands so I can see the hares running round. I describe the Northern Lights to her, but it's hard to explain exactly what it felt like, watching the sky from the beach in the middle of the night: the feeling of wonder, and the rightness of it all.

Mum stands up and goes to the window. 'We phoned Bonnie and Hannah last night,' she says. She's looking away, as if she can't bear to see my face. 'We felt we should. It didn't seem fair, you being the only one knowing about Dad and me. You should be able to talk to each other about it if you want to.'

It's another blow, soft and deadly. What had I expected? That they might have changed their minds? Decided that it wasn't too late to reconsider?

'What did they say?'

'They were both upset, of course. Bonnie especially. She wants to come home. We tried to persuade her not to. She's been having such a good time in Spain, it seems a shame to cut that short.'

'She could come here,' I say. 'I'd like that.'

'Me too.' Mum sighs. She comes back to the table and sits down. 'It's such a mess,' she says. 'So *not* what I wanted for my daughters. I'm so sorry, Kate.'

Too late, Mum. You should have thought about that before.

My anger surprises me: the way it flares up, blindingly bright and jagged like the pain over my eyes when a migraine starts.

169

She doesn't notice. We stare out of the window at the white horses on the waves. 'It's blowing up for another storm,' Mum says. 'You were lucky, catching that window of fine weather for the party.'

I yawn.

'Go and get some sleep. I don't suppose you got much last night.'

Twenty-two

I get up in the early evening. Dad comes back soon after, in time for supper. He's caught the sun: red cheeks, red nose, red neck. He looks happy though. He lists the birds he's seen. He had a chat in the café at Martinstown with a delightful young couple on their honeymoon . . .

Mum carries on folding and smoothing the washing she's brought in from the line, dried stiff by the salty wind.

Dad keeps talking. 'But all in all, I think it's probably best if I go back home this week. Lots to sort out. Should make a start.'

Mum's hands stop moving. She doesn't speak. The clock ticks round.

'So soon?' I blurt out. 'Because *I* am not going home early.'

Mum still doesn't say a word.

'Just me,' Dad says lightly, as if it doesn't matter one way or another, as if it's of no great significance. 'I wasn't expecting you to come, Kate.'

'Good. Because I'm not.'

Mum looks up at last. 'Kate?' she says. 'Could you let me and Dad have a few minutes on our own?'

I snatch up my jacket from the chair, slam the front door behind me.

The wind's blowing from the west. I walk into it, eyes stinging. I walk along the single track road and down on to the sandy beach with the fringe of marram grass along the top. I start looking for the rock shaped like a bowl that I lay in that first day on the island. Ages ago, it seems, though it's only a couple of weeks. I can't find it: the rocks all look the same from a distance.

At last I stumble across it. I climb in, lie down. Only today it doesn't feel warm, comforting, a resting place. The rock's cold, hard. Even with my collar up and my hands pulled up inside my sleeves I'm shivering. I turn on to my side, curl up. The stone cuts into my hip.

Dad's face, set hard. How could he *do* that? Simply walk away from Mum, and me, and everything we've been together as a family? Talk about it so casually, as if he doesn't care, doesn't see what he's doing to the rest of us?

The rational voice in my own head tells me it's the *only* way he could do it: a decision, and a turning away. That way he doesn't have to see the fallout. He can pretend it isn't happening, because it's all taking place somewhere else, like a shower of rain falling way out at sea. That he still, somewhere, somehow, loves us.

The one bright thought is Bonnie, on her way home.

* * *

172

It's too cold and blustery to stay still for long. I walk further along the beach, back up to the road and keep on walking westwards. The sun's going down: banks of cloud in layers building up over the sea. That's the direction the wind farm will be. I let myself imagine it: the hundreds of turbines lighting up as the sun sets: a huge forest of giant Christmas trees whirring and humming in the dark.

Maybe it's not so bad. Maybe it's a change that has to happen, and there's no point resisting.

Finn.

I imagine him and the others sitting round the table, chatting about the party, everyone helping get the dinner ready, switching on the lamps, drawing the curtains. Someone will be lighting the peat stove as the evening cools down. I think about what makes them so strong as a family. And, of course, it's Alex and Joy, their steady, loving relationship which holds it all together, invisibly. Their love for each other makes a kind of force field around them all: family, friends. It makes everyone feel safe. It keeps back the dark.

The ache inside my heart is almost unbearable tonight.

I've walked a long way: three miles at least, because I've come to the turn in the road where I waited for Finn and Isla that time before, when we went out on the bikes. Without even thinking about it I take the fork up to the white cottage. Her dad's van is parked outside, a pile of lobster pots stacked neatly by the side of the house. The wind's stronger up here: it whistles through the telephone wires, blows a trail of sand across the tarmac and on to the grass. A light's on inside the cottage.

I knock at the door. I can hear a man's voice calling out, feet coming downstairs. The door swings open and Isla's there, her hair wild round her face, her eyes blazing.

'Is he back? Is there news?' Her voice is tight with worry.

'Who?'

Disappointment floods her face.

'Who are you talking about? What's happened?' I ask.

'Finn. He hasn't come back. They've been out looking for him. I thought you must have come to tell me he's safe.'

'I don't know anything about it,' I say.

'It's been nearly eleven hours. It's getting dark. There's another storm blowing in ... it's dangerous walking along the rocks in the dark, when the tide's up. Joy has an instinct about these things. I'm surprised they didn't phone you –'

'There's no phone at our house.'

'You must have been the last person to see him, early this morning. Did he say anything? Where he was going?'

'Just that he was going to walk along to the next beach. He wanted to be by himself. He often does that, doesn't he?'

'Was he upset? Think, Kate. It's really important.'

'He was quite calm, I think . . . He listened to me, mostly, talking about things. He was nice to me.'

But he was upset about you, Isla, being with Tim –

'I suppose he was a bit preoccupied.' I take a deep breath. This is difficult to say. 'I suppose it might have been hard for him to see you and Tim getting together last night. Swimming together this morning.'

A blast of wind brings the first drops of rain.

'You'd better come in,' Isla says.

In the hall light I see her face better: embarrassed, red. She doesn't like me, I think. She blames me for something, though I can't imagine what.

Her father steps out of the kitchen, drying his hands on a towel. 'Any news?'

She shakes her head.

'You must be Kate,' he says. He shakes my hand. 'Heard about you.'

'I'll phone Joy again,' Isla says. 'It's been a while since we talked. Anything might have happened by now.'

I wait in the hall while she takes the phone and sits down on a chair to make the call. There are framed black and white photos hung along the wall and up the stairs: boats, and people. Old photos of island houses with thatched roofs and thick walls. A boy holding a large tabby cat. A group of fishermen. A younger version of Isla with hair in plaits, freckles, sitting on the top of a gate with a kite in her hands. No pictures of her mum, I notice. No sign of her. I realise for the first time that she's never referred to her mother at all.

The worry note in Isla's voice gets stronger.

I can hear another voice at the end of the line: its rising tone but not the actual words. Isla's changes, becomes reassuring. 'He'll be fine. He needed some time alone, that's all. Kate's here. Yes. She said.'

My own heartbeat quickens: I can't help it, as if worry is contagious or something. Because it seems a bit ridiculous to me, as if they are all massively over-reacting. Unless there's something they all know about Finn. Something I don't know.

Isla puts her hand over the mouthpiece and turns to me. 'What were you talking about with Finn? You said he just listened.'

My turn to go red. 'About me, and a boy called Sam. And about a car accident I was in. But nothing too terrible, honestly. And Finn was very calm and wise. He didn't seem upset by it. Not at all.'

She goes back to her call. I'm trying to hear both sides of the conversation but it's impossible. She just says things like *yes, no, I don't think so. Just friends. Yes.*

The clock on the wall ticks round. Ten fifteen. Dusk outside. Wind rattling the door.

'What was he wearing?' Isla's asking me.

I try to remember. 'Jeans. Black T-shirt. Grey top, I think, tied round his waist. Boots.'

But no coat. No waterproofs . . .

He knows this island as well as anybody. There are plenty of places to take shelter. That ruined house where I waited for the rain to stop. Old barns. Boat-houses. The old chapel. He's probably called in on someone; been invited in for supper, just forgotten to let anyone know. They are usually all so relaxed and casual about time at the Manse that I'm surprised they even noticed that Finn hadn't come home. There must be something else. There has to be. Otherwise, it doesn't add up.

Isla puts the phone back. Her dad comes into the hall again. 'Well?' he asks.

'No, he still isn't back.' She frowns. 'Where might he go? Any ideas, Kate?'

'I've no idea. You know him much better than I do, Isla.'

'Yes.' She sounds irritated. Or maybe afraid.

Her dad reaches for his coat, picks up his keys from the hall table. 'We'll go over to the Manse,' he says. 'See where they've looked already. Give them a hand. We can drop you off on the way, Kate. It's getting late.'

There's no room to argue. Isla climbs into the back of the van and I go in the front seat next to her dad. The van stinks of fish, salt water, the sharp, clean smell of metal.

It's properly dark now, and the clouds make it darker still. We rattle down the track, back along the coast road next to the dunes towards the village. The telephone kiosk is illuminated: a box of light in the dark. The silhouette of a man talking animatedly into the phone is in plain view. My heart sinks. Dad.

Isla's father brakes and pulls up on the grass. 'There you go, Kate. Get some sleep. We'll let you know if there's any news about the lad.'

'Thanks,' I say.

He pulls the van door behind me and it clicks firmly shut. It's clear to me that I've been dismissed. Not needed. Not wanted. Islanders, closing ranks.

I watch the van drive down through the village, over the cattle grid, past the telecom mast and the shop, and the red tail lights fade into the darkness. I can't bear to go inside the house where Mum will be waiting, alone. Dad still hasn't seen me luckily: he's too intent on whoever he's talking to. *Her*, I guess: the woman. So instead of walking in, I go straight past the house, cutting across the grass and behind the shop to rejoin the road the other side.

Keep walking.

The west wind is sweeping the heavy clouds over the island and away. The rain will fall elsewhere this time. Every so often there's a clear patch of sky, enough to glimpse stars, planets, a slice of moon.

Where would Finn go, if he was wanting to hide? Somewhere special to him, that felt safe.

Collay, I think. That island where we collected cockles.

The idea of him rowing across the water in the dark, in the wind, makes me sick to my stomach. He wouldn't be so stupid. Would he? Please not . . . But, of course, he might have gone over while it was still light, and then the tide would have come in and he would have had to stay there. That would explain everything.

Surely someone would have thought of that already; checked if the boat was missing?

I keep walking into the dark.

I should have gone with him, this morning. I nearly did. If he'd looked as if he'd wanted me to, I would have. But maybe that's the whole point. When people can't reach out, that might be when they need you most. You have to be brave enough to push past the closed-off facade . . .

This morning! It seems impossible that this is still the same day.

In my head I suddenly hear Finn's voice, as loud and clear as if he were standing in front of me. *The ringing stone*. That first time we ran along the beach together, me huffing and sweating and out of breath. A special place, that's been there for thousands of years. And it seems more and more possible, the more I think about it. It's too far from the road for anyone in a car or jeep to have seen him. You'd have to clamber along the rocky shoreline, take a path across fields, along the cliff . . . I try to remember details from the map on the wall in the museum.

Now I've got a purpose, a place to head to, I feel much more confident. I convince myself that I'll be the one to find him, when no one else has. Perhaps Isla doesn't know him as well as she thinks she does. It's as if I'm being guided by some sort of animal instinct. Thinking the way Finn might. I try to remember more. Past the ruined house, and the field of black cattle, along past the Iron Age fort, called a *broch*, and the Neolithic cairns . . .

The sound of the sea crashing on to the sand is louder at night. Most of the birds have already roosted, but every so often I hear the lonely call of a curlew or something, echoing across the bay. The light at the end of the pier blinks on, off, on. It shines out across the heaving water. I pull my collar up and put my hands deep in my pockets. The temperature's dropped. Just as well I am walking fast.

It seems as if it's all I've done for weeks now: walking. You'd think I'd know this small island like the back of my hand, but I still don't and everything looks different at night. At the church, I take the left fork that takes me across the island at its narrowest point. Not a single car passes me the whole way. The scattered houses are all in darkness, as if everyone is asleep.

At last the ruined house looms ahead, and beyond that, North Bay. The sea is calm this side of the island, out of the wind. I take the narrow path that runs above the beach, round the coast. It's so dark and silent that I feel I must walk as quietly as I can too, but even so, I startle a bird and it rises up squawking, flapping its big wings as it wheels away.

The clouds are clearing: the patches of starlit sky get bigger, and when the path comes out on to the cliff I glimpse the moon again: a bright silver crescent, already higher in the sky.

I have to pick my way between boulders; the path seems to peter out altogether in places, and then I come out on to a broad spread of cropped grass divided in two by a running stream, a wooden bridge across, and a single house: a traditional one with deep walls and a tarred roof. The windows are shuttered. *Imagine living here.*

I keep going. The rocks are craggy ahead, dark shapes against the sky: the cairns, possibly, or the outline of the *broch*. No signposts or anything to help. All I want now is to find him, for it all to be OK. *And then sleep.*

But it begins to feel ridiculous, the chances of him being out here. Why was I so confident before?

And what if . . . what exactly might I find, if I *do* find him? Dark thoughts, conjured up by the darkness, swarm in my mind.

Twenty-three

It's much harder going now; I can't see far enough ahead to find the path easily. I have to guess where to step, find myself sliding between huge rocks, slipping into patches of bog. The stench of marsh gas is everywhere. I keep remembering fragments of stories about people sucked down and suffocating in thick mud . . . the poems about the sacrificial corpses . . . I work out that the trick is to step on the clumps of reeds; if you look carefully you can see the gleam of moonlight reflected off the bog water in between. All the time, the sea's creeping closer, splashing on to rocks: it must be nearly high tide.

I slip, lose my balance, cry out. I'm up to one knee in stinking black mud. *Stupid. This is stupid now. Just go back.* Hot tears on my cheeks. I stop for a moment, sit down on the edge of one of the boulders so I can catch my breath, wipe the mud off my jeans and shoe. My heart's thudding.

I make myself look up, up to the open sky. *Don't*

give up, I tell myself, and sitting there, my back against the rock, one foot wet and slimy with mud, I find I'm staring at the stars and thinking of Sam again. The real Sam I glimpsed, who no one else seemed to recognise. What would he have made of a place like this? Skies like this? Doesn't he deserve a second chance? Maybe Finn was wrong about him.

I hear something. The crunch of feet on shingle.

I freeze. Someone's out there, just below my rocky outcrop. How long have they been there? Who is it?

My palms are clammy. I wait. Can they see me? I peer into the dark at the silhouette.

Can it be? I let my eyes adjust to the dim light. And yes – I'm sure of it now – it really is Finn. He's crouching down, picking up stones on the scrap of beach. I watch him for a while, even though it seems wrong – but how do I suddenly let him know I'm here, now, without scaring him half to death? And then I start wondering if he's hoping to be found, secretly wishing for someone to come looking for him, to bring him home, like me when I was little, too well hidden in a game of hide-and-seek, longing for Bonnie or Hannah to find me at last.

I shift slightly on my rocky perch and a dislodged stone rolls away, drops on to the beach below. The sound makes Finn stop in his tracks.

'Finn?' I call softly. 'It's me. Kate.'

He swings round, sees me above him. 'What on earth are you doing here?'

'Looking for you, of course. Everyone is. They're all worried about you, for some reason.'

He doesn't say anything for a while. He hunkers down on the pebbles, as if it's perfectly normal to be beachcombing along the tideline in the dark.

I wait. I'm shivering.

'How come you knew I'd be here?' he asks.

'I didn't,' I say. 'But I had this hunch, about the ringing stone . . . You told me about it once.'

He looks towards me, but I can't see his expression from up here.

'So very clever, Kate,' he says. He stands up and stretches out his back as if it's aching.

'Why are they worried?' he says, as if the thought had genuinely not occurred to him. 'I'm surprised they even noticed.'

'Joy and Alex notice everything,' I say. 'Of course, they would notice you hadn't come home all day. Isla's been anxious too.'

'Hah!'

'Seriously. It was Isla who told me you hadn't come back all day. And she and her dad have gone to the Manse to help look for you. So, you have to come back with me now.' I make myself sound more forceful than I really feel.

He carries on scooping up stones, letting them go. A noise a bit like jangling coins: that thing Dad does when he's nervous.

'What have you been doing all this time, anyway?' I ask.

'Thinking,' Finn says. 'Making plans.'

'In the dark.'

'Yes. While it is properly dark, as opposed to lit up by three hundred turbines.'

'And?'

'I've worked it out. What we need to do.'

I realise I'm so cold my teeth are chattering. 'Can we talk about it on the way back?' I say.

'All right. But not before you've actually seen the ringing stone,' Finn says.

I humour him. 'OK. Show me the stone. Then we're going back. And you can tell me your plan.' I climb down on to the pebbles.

He steps forward and puts his arms right round me.

It takes me completely by surprise.

He mumbles something into my hair I can't hear.

'What?' I say, speaking into his jumper. It feels so very lovely, being held close. I wish we could stay like that, his arms tight round me, for a long, long time. And maybe he feels the same. We both sigh deeply, as if we are finally relaxing and letting go.

'That's better,' Finn says into my hair.

'Yes,' I mumble back, my face still squashed into his chest.

It really does feel better. Surprisingly so.

'Thank you,' he says, finally letting go and stepping back. 'For bothering. For coming to look for me. The way you pay attention and listen to things. It's good, that.'

I could be embarrassed, but I choose not to be. It's such a relief to find he's all right; so kind of normal.

Finn's sort of normal, I mean. We don't kiss or anything. I know it's Isla he wants really, not me, and this is just friendship. But it's the real kind, and I know it will last. The thought makes me happy.

'Come on, then,' he says. 'I'll show you the stone. It isn't far.'

'Good,' I say. 'I'm exhausted. I've been walking for ever, it seems like.'

He takes my hand and leads me along the beach and up between rocks, weaving in and out, over boulders and across a series of small streams – *fresh water springs*, Finn says – in a small sloping field above the sea.

The stone doesn't look anything special, except for the cup-shaped marks, and I'd never have noticed those in the dark. We run our hands over the dents to feel the shapes worn away by the hands of people who lived here thousands of years ago.

'The story is,' Finn says, 'that if this stone breaks in two the island will be lost. It will sink beneath the sea.' He cups his hands around mine for a second. 'I suppose it might, if sea levels carry on rising. Global warming and all that.'

It's one of the arguments for wind energy: the need to stop using the fossil fuels that are warming the planet. It's one of the reasons why the wind farm idea is so confusing, because Finn knows that we have to do *something* about energy: we can't go on burning fossil fuels, guzzling oil or gas like we all do, as if it doesn't matter.

'So,' he says. 'My plan. Maybe we can't stop the

wind farm. But if they do go ahead and build it, we have to make sure it's much, much further out at sea. At least thirty-five miles or so away from the island.'

'Really?' I say.

'I still think it's a huge, expensive mistake, mind. I've been thinking about it over and over, all day, trying to work out what case to make. And finally, when I was just sitting here this evening watching the divers, it came to me. Like a sudden gift. The whole thing. I've worked it all out.' His face looks so different: animated, his eyes shining.

'So, what have the divers got to do with it? What are they diving for, exactly? Is there sunken treasure: a wreck? Or pearls, or what?'

He laughs. 'Not *people* divers. Birds. Great northern divers. They spend the winter here – but they're very rare, a protected species, so we can make a case for the sea around the island needing to be protected on environmental grounds. There are rare corncrakes too, and all the migrating birds. There are laws about this stuff already. SPAs. Special protected areas. We'll have to get all the facts together but I am sure we can make a case. I don't know why we didn't think of it before.'

I like how he says *we*. He assumes I'm on his side.

I really try to pay attention to everything he's explaining, but I'm so tired, so cold, it's all I can do to stay standing upright.

'That's great, Finn,' I say eventually. '*Now* can we go back?'

'Make the stone ring,' he says. He hands me one of the pebbles from the beach. 'Just hit it against the stone.'

He laughs at my feeble attempt. 'Again, but much harder!'

With a bit of imagination, maybe it does sound like a bell ringing out. A soft, muffled bell. But it would be the same with any two stones, wouldn't it? I don't tell him that. Maybe there is something special about it, after all. Because something's changed in Finn, anyone can see that.

We walk back along the cliff the way we came. When the path's wide enough for us to be side by side, he turns to look at me. His face is pale in the moonlight. 'I disappeared once before. For five days, from boarding school. Last year. That must be why they were all worrying about me today. Just so you know.'

'Why on earth didn't you tell me that before?'

He shrugs. 'It's over and done with. That's why. In the past. I want to forget about all that now.'

I'm too tired to argue. I link my arm with his, and we walk slowly back, stepping over stones, finding the clumps of sedge and reeds over the marshy places. I feel the warmth of his side against mine, and when we have to climb over the boulders to get back on to the narrow footpath he places his hand in the small of my back, to help me up. In my exhausted state, almost sleepwalking now, I let myself wonder what it would be like, to be properly close to Finn, to be the person he tells the really important stuff to. I can almost imagine, in my dreaming state of mind, how it would be. Something more than friendship . . .

It seems such a very long way back, but at last we're at the edge of the bay, and on to the single-track road, and there's a car – headlights – the taxi, I see now, slowing down and stopping. The door's opening and Alex is running towards us, calling Finn's name.

Twenty—four

In the past. That's what Finn said.

But the past doesn't stay in the past, does it?

I'm lying in bed, half awake, running over in my head everything that's happened in the last twenty-four hours.

The walk home with Finn's all a bit of a blur: me stumbling over my feet, tired to the core, and Finn still talking about corncrakes and terns and divers, as if it was normal to be walking back at night talking about birds, as if there wasn't a whole family – and lots of friends – anxious about him back at the Manse, scared he's disappeared again.

The moment when we saw the headlights coming slowly towards us – Alex at the wheel of the old taxi – the hugs and then the awkward silence on the way back to my place, because Alex insisted they drop me home first.

Mum and Dad waiting up for me, cross and relieved at the same time. And the news that Bonnie is already on her way: she'll be coming on the ferry on Friday.

Dad was talking to *Bonnie* on the phone last night when I saw him in the kiosk . . .

It's nearly midday. I've slept all this time. The smell of peat smoke drifts upstairs. Someone's lit the stove in the sitting room. I think of the neat peat stack at the Manse, the turves laid in layers up the side of the house, arranged in the traditional herringbone pattern: the handiwork of Finn, Piers and Jamie. Three brothers, like an echo of us three sisters: me, Bonnie and Hannah . . .

I think about that bright, breezy day up on the peat banks, talking to Tim, helping get the sack loads of peat into the jeep. Finn's spade cutting down into dark brown seams of peat, the layers of grass roots laid down over hundreds and thousands of years . . . Finn slicing it in blocks like chocolate and stacking it to dry in the sun and the wind . . . The skylarks singing their hearts out, rising higher and higher into the sky, and Piers and Clara reciting lines of poetry about the Highland girl. The dark stories about the man found in the bog, perfectly preserved, a noose round his neck and the grains of seed still in his belly . . .

The past doesn't stay past, not in a landscape and not in people either. Because we are the sum of all the things that have happened to us, or that we've made happen. It's a living, breathing part of who we are, all of us. It goes on living in us. All the happy things that have happened, and all the sad ones too.

My head spins with thinking about all this, but I'm not so anxious or angry any more, I realise; not like when we first arrived at the house. Something has settled in me; a rich dark seam of experience, I suppose, being laid down, and other new ones on top, gradually covering up the pain.

I hear a car slow down and pull up near the house: a knock at the door, and Mum's voice, talking to someone. I strain to hear who it is.

'Still asleep,' Mum says. 'No. OK. I'll tell her. Thanks. So glad to hear that . . .'

A car door slams. The car drives away. I could get up, go and look to see who it was – Alex or Piers perhaps, or maybe Tim, on his way to Isla's house – but I'm still sleepy, and my legs still ache.

I'm determined to ask Finn what happened to him before, what made him go off, where he went. But not today . . .

I slip back into sleep.

At some point in the afternoon Dad appears in the bedroom doorway. He's wearing his coat; I know instantly what he's come to say, even though I'm still groggy with sleep.

'I'm just saying goodbye,' he says. 'I hoped you'd be up before this; I could have talked to you properly. But the ferry's nearly in. I need to dash.'

'Bye, Dad.' I swallow a great gulp of sadness.

He steps right into the little room, leans over and kisses the top of my head. 'I'll see you back at home,' he says. 'We'll start sorting things out. Please don't worry, darling. Love you.'

And with that he's gone.

* * *

I watch the light change in the square of window above my bed. Clouds scurry across; at one point a squall of rain hits the glass. It clears again. Through the small window at the front of the room, I see the sea, grey waves topped with white. I drift in and out of sleep, dreams, thoughts. I have to go to the loo eventually: it's the only thing that will make me get up. It's quiet downstairs: Mum must have gone with Dad to the ferry. I imagine her waving him off, the tears on her cheeks. This particular goodbye is just the first of a whole series, taking him further away from our lives . . . out of hers for ever maybe.

I get dressed. My legs are still aching from the walking yesterday, and stiff from being in bed too long. I take my jacket from the hook, stuff my feet into my walking boots, go outside. The wind snatches the door, buffets me in the face. I put my hood up, shove my hands into my pockets, set my back to the wind.

The ferry's already left the harbour: it's ploughing across the Sound, appearing and disappearing in the swell and spray. It edges along the coast to make the most of the shelter, before it sets out over the open water.

I meet Mum coming back up the road from the ferry, head bent against the wind, her face red. She doesn't see me until I'm close up. I hug her; she holds on to me, tight.

'Shall we get a coffee?' Mum says. 'I can't face going back to the house, not yet.'

The café's warm inside; the windows are all steamed

up. We order coffee and hot chocolate, and we sit together at a table with a bright red tablecloth, hands round the shiny red mugs. We don't say much but it feels comforting sitting there together. Around us, families talk and drink tea and children squabble: just a normal day.

'We'll be fine,' Mum says.

'Yes,' I say.

'We'll get used to it.'

'Yes.'

She laughs, a hollow laugh. 'Plenty more fish in the sea.'

'Oh, Mum.' I could cry buckets, but for her sake I won't.

'Let's hope the weather picks up again. Everything's more bearable when the sun shines.'

I reach across the table and squeeze her hand. 'I'm glad we're staying, anyway.'

'Really?' Her face brightens. 'You don't hate it here? Hate me for making you come?'

'No!' I say. 'It's an incredible place. I'm having an amazing time. Honestly. Now, I understand why you wanted to come back here so much. And we won't let Dad spoil it for us.'

'You sound more grown-up than I do,' Mum says.

I don't answer.

'Did someone call round earlier?' I ask her after a while.

'Yes, sorry, I was meant to tell you. A young man called Tim. Very handsome!'

'What did he say?'

'That everything's fine at the Manse – Finn's well, and to say thank you for finding him, and that he – Tim – is going to the mainland for a couple of days – in fact, he'll be gone already. He'll have been on the same ferry as your dad. Who is he, exactly?'

'One of Finn's brothers' friends.'

'The one who had the beach party?'

'Yes.'

Mum sips her coffee. 'So, tell me some more about Finn. Did you find out why he went off like that?'

'Not really. He seems to need time away from people – he goes off to think. He gets upset about stuff, and then he needs to be alone for a bit, to sort things out in his head. And maybe he was upset about Tim and Isla getting together at the party. *He* didn't admit that, mind.'

'Isla?'

'She lives here. Her dad's a fisherman. She's pretty, with auburn hair.'

Mum nods, as if she's taking it all in. I know she's miles away really.

'Anyway, Finn didn't mean to worry everyone. I don't think he had any idea they'd be so anxious. But it seems he's disappeared before, which is why they reacted like that yesterday.'

Mum's quiet, thinking. She looks at me. 'We've not talked much about Sam, have we? Are you over him now?'

I'm immediately defensive. '*Over* him? Like forgotten about him, you mean?'

'No, no, I didn't mean that, Kate. I know how important a first boyfriend is.'

'Really?' I look at her.

She smiles. 'Of course. You never forget the first one. But I'm sad for you, that you can't have happy memories of Sam . . .'

'Don't say that! I do have happy memories. You don't even know him. It wasn't like him – how he was that night –'

Mum can't stop herself interrupting. 'It was shocking. Truly terrible. He could have killed you. And the woman in the other car. The people in the car behind even. Nothing can excuse that behaviour.'

'I know that.'

'You do?' She seems surprised.

'I've had lots of time to think about it,' I say. 'It was really scary. And I will never understand why he did what he did. I know he was unpredictable sometimes. But he was really lovely too. He listened to me. Cared about me. He talked to me about things like the stars and the world and science. He's really intelligent. I know if he'd had a better start then things would be different for him now –'

'Oh, Kate!' Mum sighs. 'But you can see how worried it made me and Dad, can't you? That night, you not coming home and it getting later and later and then finally that phone call, from the police . . . You can imagine what we thought.'

'I know. I'm sorry, Mum.'

Her eyes fill with tears. 'All we want is for you to be safe and happy – and I know how ironic that sounds, with everything that's happening now – but it's the truth, Kate.' She squeezes my hand. 'You do know that? How much we love you?'

I nod.

'Good.'

'So,' I say, 'can we talk about something else now? Not Sam, or Finn, or Dad? No boys or men at all.'

'All right.' She smiles. 'Yes, I'll try.'

We sit in silence.

'OK,' I say. 'Complete change of subject. What do you know about Special Protection Areas? For birds, habitats, that sort of thing?'

'Nothing at all,' Mum says. 'Why?'

'It's the next stage for our campaign.'

'I didn't know there was a campaign. For what?'

'Saving the island from the wind farm.'

Mum looks even more confused.

'Where've you *been*, Mum! The issue everyone on the island is talking about! The thing that might change this amazing place for ever if we don't do something about it!'

'Sorry,' Mum says. 'I guess I've been a bit preoccupied with my own personal tragedy.'

'Well, never mind,' I say. 'You can catch up now. I might go to that community centre place and look it all up on the internet. Not today though.' I stir the sugary sludge at the bottom of my mug.

Mum's staring absentmindedly at other tables in the café. A family bickering about something. A couple holding hands across a table. A little girl with a dog on a lead sitting next to an elderly man.

The café man nods in our direction. 'Everything OK?'

Mum comes to. She nods back. 'Yes thanks, Ken.'

'I know,' she says to me. 'We'll stop at the shop on the way home and choose ourselves a lovely supper. Well, as lovely as that shop allows. What do you fancy?'

'Lamb chops, new potatoes and beans. And fresh raspberries with cream for afters.'

Mum doesn't make the connection, and I don't tell her. It's the meal Dad cooked for us, on the first day of the holiday. I think of him, alone, making his way back without us.

'Before we shop, do you mind if we walk up to the little hill above the village? So I can check my phone for messages?' Mum asks.

'Good idea,' I say. 'I haven't checked mine for ages.'

Strange, how quickly you get out of the habit. To begin with, I thought I'd *die* without my phone.

The cool air is a shock after the steamy café. I turn up my collar. We walk side by side out of the village, past the post office and over the second cattle grid, up the small hill.

My phone bleeps in my pocket. I check my inbox.

Three texts. Bonnie, Hannah, Molly.

One missed call.

I check the details. My heart skips a beat: the missed call was from Sam.

My hands are shaking. I click on voicemail.

His voice. It sounds so odd, hearing it here, on the island. *Sorry for everything. You OK? Hope so.*

I check the date and time he sent it.

Days ago.

My heart's racing. Finn said I should forget Sam

– just *make the decision*, he said. And that's what Mum wants me to do. But it's what's always happened to Sam: people giving up, not bothering about him. Is that what I'm going to do too? I listen again, and then while I'm working out what to say back I open the messages from my sisters. They're both gutted about Mum and Dad. Worried about me. Bonnie's on her way . . .

Reading their texts makes me realise how, already, I am beginning to adjust; that it's not so raw and awful as it was even a few days ago; how everything changes so fast.

I'm OK, I text. **Glad I'm here with Mum. Xxx**

I send it to Bonnie and Hannah.

Molly says she's missing me, but having a great holiday. They are camping in Cornwall and it's been sunny every single day so far. She'll see me back at school in September.

I listen to Sam's voice again. I start writing a text, but the words won't come. Nothing seems right. I don't send anything in the end.

Mum's already walking back to the village. I run down after her. 'Wait for me!' I call after her.

Over supper, we talk about how we are going to manage the rest of the holidays. Mum thinks we should have a big dinner and invite all our new friends – everyone at the Manse, and her friend Fiona, and other people she's met.

'You're not the only one making new island friends,' she says when I look surprised.

'Let's wait for Bonnie to be here,' I say. 'Tim might be back by then too.'

'And?' Mum says. 'The connection between those things is?' She laughs. 'I wonder what Bonnie would say to you!'

'She'd be pleased I was thinking about her best interests,' I say. 'Tim is lovely. Most of the time.'

We make a list. We add Isla and her dad; Mackie, and the other man who helped with the jeep: Rob. He's more like Mum's age.

We put more peat on the stove. Draw the curtains, turn on the telly. There's nothing much on so we watch one of the DVDs from my room instead.

'You choose,' Mum says.

'*My Summer of Love*,' I say.

Mum pulls a face.

'It's about two girls,' I tell her. 'So we'll be fine.'

Mum makes us tea and we drink it from the hare cups. We snuggle side by side on the leather sofa; Mum gets a rug from her bedroom to tuck round us. It's almost cosy, just the two of us.

Twenty–five

Wednesday 14th August. The island has a different feel today. Even the air smells different. The sky is blue, but a different blue, more transparent, as if the air is thinner. Summer is shorter up here, or perhaps it simply starts earlier. The school holidays are different to ours too. Their Autumn term starts in mid-August rather than September, which explains why the blue school bus is whizzing along the island road first thing, picking up small groups of children along the way.

I watch it through the open front window in my pyjamas, cradling an early cup of tea. I'd no idea there were so many children living on the island. Where have they been all summer? Perhaps they take their holidays elsewhere . . .

A thought strikes me: Isla will be back at school this morning. My mood lifts. I don't know why. Is it because last time I saw her, I felt she didn't like me much? As if it was my fault that Finn went off. Anyway, if she's at school all day, there's less chance of seeing her. And Finn won't be moping about, wondering whether he's going to bump into her and Tim. Only Tim isn't around either – it seems he had work to do on the mainland. He'll be back on the Friday boat.

Mum joins me at the window. 'Can you imagine going to school here?' she asks.

'Yes,' I say, 'I actually can.'

'Really?'

I shrug. 'Why not? It would be a small school, but that would be cool. You'd know everyone. Easy to get to: the bus picks you up. And after school you could go straight down to the beach.'

Mum laughs. 'What's happened to you, Kate?'

'Your island magic, I guess,' I say.

Mum sighs heavily. 'Shame it didn't work on your dad,' she says.

'We're not talking about him, remember?' I say.

'Still? For how long?' Mum asks.

'For however long it takes. Till we both feel fine again.'

'You are such an inspiration,' Mum says suddenly. 'I don't know what I'd do without you.'

'Aw, Mum!' I hug her. 'That's nice. But in reality, you'd be fine even if I wasn't here.'

She doesn't look convinced. 'It's such a big thing, starting all over again, at my age. I never, ever thought this would happen to us.'

'You're not that old,' I tell her. 'And new starts are good, aren't they? Like a chance to do things differently, or do things you never did before. It might even be exciting!'

She shivers. 'Maybe. Given time.'

'I'm going to cycle to the community centre this morning,' I say. 'I want to use the computers there.'

'Good idea,' Mum says. 'I'm going to sort things out here, tidy up a bit. Plan the dinner for Friday. I might have a walk later, if the sun stays out.'

You have to pay to use the computers, so I do a very quick search about the birds, and protected areas and print out the relevant pages to show Finn later. I check Facebook and emails before the money runs out: Molly's posted photos from Cornwall, and I read the updates on Bonnie's blog from Spain, but apart from that I've not missed anything really. It's weird how loads of things which seemed so important when I was at home have all dropped away since I've been here.

The community café is almost empty: I have to ring the bell at the counter and wait for someone to come and serve me.

A middle-aged bloke with scruffy hair and a beard appears after a while. 'Sorry,' he says. 'Just got off the morning ferry. Catching up with things. What can I get you? Coffee? Tea?'

'Tea, please,' I say.

He fills an old-fashioned kettle, takes a china teapot down from a shelf, lays a tray with a cup and saucer. 'Have a free cake,' he says, opening up a plastic box. 'I made them at the weekend: they got a bit squashed on the way back.'

I pick out a cupcake with pink and white icing. 'Thanks,' I say.

He disappears out the back again. I settle down at the window table where I sat before with Finn. I read through the pages from the environment site. It looks promising: there's lots of evidence already about the importance of the island as a habitat for loads of rare birds: the divers, but also corncrakes, and redshanks, ringed plovers . . .

'Hey, Kate!'

Finn's standing right in front of me.

'Talk of the devil,' I say. 'What are you doing here?'

'I called at yours. Your mum said you'd be here.'

'I've been researching your birds.'

'Thanks!' he says, sitting down opposite me. 'I've done the same thing. Found masses of stuff. We've definitely got a case.'

He tells me that more than forty-two per cent of the British population of the great northern divers have their wintering grounds here. 'That's way over the numbers you need to make a case for an SPA. The fact that no one else has even mentioned it suggests there's been some sort of cover-up.'

I laugh. 'You're so suspicious!'

'You're not?'

'Well, what are we going to do about it?'

'Get the facts. Send lots of letters. Get a proper campaign off the ground.'

'I've been thinking too,' I say. 'You should put together your own exhibition, about all the things you love about this place. Photos of the rare birds and the amazing beaches and quiet roads and the peat beds and crofts and all the things that would disappear if the wind farm came too close. The traditions of farming and fishing and all that. We could take loads of stunning photos. Write about it. Collect stuff . . . I don't know, maybe record sounds, like a sound poem or something – bird calls and the sound of the sea and the wind blowing through the fields of barley, and people talking about what they love about living here . . .' My voice falters. 'Why are you looking at me like that?'

'Because you're a genius,' Finn says. 'And I've never heard you say so much in one go!' He laughs. 'It's a brilliant idea. Tim's right, calling you *clever* Kate!'

I blush.

Finn doesn't notice. He pushes his chair back. 'Don't know why I didn't think of doing something like this before. Guess I've not really been thinking straight. Got too gloomy.'

'We should get everyone involved,' I say. 'Even people like Mackie, and Isla's dad, as well as your family.' I'm getting even more carried away now, ideas spinning round my brain. 'Tim's always wanted to do broadcast journalism; this could be his chance. And your brothers could compose music – an island symphony or something. We could ask the museum people to help, and the school. Isla – we have to have Isla, because she belongs here properly, she was born here. Her voice counts for more than any of us . . .'

It's Finn's turn to blush. 'Of course, Isla.'

'I'll help a bit,' I say quickly. 'I've only got another week here, but I can help you get started. When do you have to go back to school?'

Finn gets up without answering. He rings the bell

205

at the counter and orders a coffee for himself. I watch him. What have I gone and said now? He's so oversensitive. Was it me mentioning Isla?

He comes back and sits down. He runs his hand through his hair. 'I don't think I am.'

'What?'

'I'm not going back.'

I wait for him to explain. He doesn't speak for ages. He sips his coffee, I pour another cup of tea.

'I had a long talk with my parents,' he says. 'About the time I went off before, and how much I hate being at boarding school, and all that. And they said I can stay here. Don't have to go back to finish A levels at school if I really can't stand it. And I can't. So I'm going to live here, get a job of some kind. I can always go to the island school later if I change my mind about getting exams.'

'You lucky thing!' I say. 'Your parents are amazing. What did you say to convince them?'

'I talked about what I really feel, being away. Boarding. And about what makes me happy. And they listened, and at last they understood.'

'Have you told Isla?'

'Not yet. I haven't seen her.'

'The thing with Tim won't last,' I say.

He looks up. 'What makes you say that?'

I shrug. 'Just a feeling. He's gone over to the mainland for a few days. And he'll have to go back to work properly soon. Out of sight, out of mind. And now you'll be here all the year round!' I smile at him, teasing. 'How could she possibly resist?'

I look at his red face. 'You two are meant for each other, Finn. It's obvious. She just hasn't seen it yet, but she will.'

Bonnie's a much more sensible age for Tim. I don't tell Finn that, but it's what I realised ages ago. Not that I'm matchmaking, not really . . . and Tim's not the sensible responsible person I first thought he was, so maybe he wouldn't be right for Bonnie either.

'What job will you get?' I say.

'We're planning to start farming the croft properly, me and Alex,' Finn says. 'Start with a few sheep, chickens. Grow some vegetables. And maybe I'll get an apprenticeship with one of the island builders, or learn to do plumbing or something useful.'

'It's such a good plan,' I tell him. 'It seems absolutely the right thing for you.'

He smiles at me. He suddenly looks so happy I can't resist leaning over and giving him a kiss.

'What's that about?' he says.

'I'm happy for you,' I say. 'That's all.'

We cycle back to the village together; Finn asks me back to his house for tea. I call in at home to tell Mum where I'll be. Dad's old camera is hanging from one of the coat pegs in the hall: I pick it up to show Finn. 'Let's practise taking photos,' I say, 'all the way to the Manse.'

We take it in turns, stopping along the road to take photos of the things we pass: traditional thatched houses with thick walls; two ruined chapels; a wooden gate tied with blue string and the blue sea behind. I laugh at Finn when he lies right down on the machair to photograph bees on wild flowers at eye level. He does the same with the dune grass blowing in the wind, catching the pattern of light and shade. We leave the bikes at the top of the beach and walk out along a finger of rock, photographing rock pools, interesting rock formations and colours, a washed-up lobster pot. I try to take a panoramic view of the wide bay: the expanse of sea and sky and wind-whipped clouds that I've grown to love so much. We cycle slowly on to the Manse. Finally we get there, park up the bikes. Finn photographs the two bikes leaning in together, against a backdrop of wall and peat stack.

Joy smiles as we come in to the kitchen. 'You look cheerful,' she says to Finn.

He tells her about our plan. He shows her the photos on the camera.

'Not bad,' she says. 'Not bad at all.'

'Can we borrow your laptop?' Finn asks.

'Go right ahead. It's on my desk, under a pile of papers.'

Our pictures look even better on the laptop screen. Finn's are a million times better than mine. He sees things differently: his are all more focused, closer up: the detail of a wild flower or a shell or the strange patterns made by tides on the sand. The close-up of the bee is amazing; you can even see the crumbs of pollen on its furry back.

'We'll need to get photos of those diving birds,' I say, 'seeing as they are crucial for getting the special protected area thing.'

I leave the camera with him when it's time for me to go back. 'It's Dad's,' I tell him. 'He left it behind. Mum won't even notice. You can bring it back when you all come over to ours for supper on Friday.'

Joy says she's looking forward to meeting Mum. 'And it will be lovely to see one of your sisters again. I wonder if Piers and Jamie will remember her?'

On the way back I stop at the hill to check my phone. No new messages. At last, I send my reply to Sam.

You'd love this northern sky, and the stars you can see here: you should come, one day. I've even seen the aurora borealis! Hope you're OK. Miss you. Kate

Twenty–six

The wind's stronger than ever on Thursday. Mum and I listen to the shipping forecast: force 8 winds expected later.

'Bonnie might not make it tomorrow,' Mum says. 'We'd better change the big dinner to Saturday, just in case the ferry doesn't run. Would you cycle round and tell everyone, please?'

'What! That's miles!' I say. 'It'll take me hours! Who have you invited, anyway?'

She shows me her list. 'Anyone else you want to add?'

My mind keeps flitting to Dad, far away and missing us. Because I bet he is. I bet he goes on missing us. I bet he'll never really *not* miss us, however much he pretends otherwise.

I set off on the bike after lunch. The wind's blowing from the west, so I cycle to the Manse first, with the wind behind me. I lean the bike against the wall.

Joy's in the garden, trying to peg the washing to the line. The wind tugs at the sheet as she pegs the corners, blows it out and then flaps it back so it wraps round her like a white cloak. She laughs as a pillow-case whips free and blows across the garden. 'Catch it for me!' she calls.

I run after it, snatch it up and put it back in the basket.

'He's on the computer,' Joy says through the peg in her mouth. 'Just go right in.'

'It's you I came to see, actually.' I tell her about Saturday. 'I'm going round the island to tell everyone about the change.'

'Why don't you leave the list of people with me?' Joy says. 'I can phone everyone in a fraction of the time it will take you on that old boneshaker! Unless you really *want* a long bike ride, of course?'

I laugh. 'No. Not really. It'll take me hours.'

'And extra hard work in this wind,' Joy says.

I help her hang out the rest of the clothes in the basket. We go inside together.

Joy smoothes her hair back where it's come undone. She starts over again, uncoiling and shaking out her long grey hair before retwisting it, pinning it back up. Her face is pink from the wind and sun, her eyes bright. She's happy in her own skin, I think. She doesn't fuss about how she looks. This is how Isla will be when she's Joy's age. I feel a little pang of envy.

Joy's filling the kettle and putting mugs on a tray. 'He's so much happier now he's got a plan,' she says.

'Finn?'

211

'Yes, Finn.'

'He seems really happy he doesn't have to go back to school,' I say.

'Well, we'll see,' Joy says. 'The grass is always greener – you know? It's not an easy life, farming. He has an awful lot to learn. He might be bored out of his skull, living with his aged parents all the time.'

But I know he won't be. He's got what he most wanted, after all.

'And how are *you*, Kate?' Joy asks, out of the blue. 'I'm sorry about your dad leaving, I really am.'

I take a deep breath.

'It's very hard, but I'm going to be OK,' I tell her. 'Being on the island has helped me in so many ways. I didn't expect that. But I love it here now. Meeting Finn, and all of you – well, it's made a big difference to me.'

Joy hugs me. 'I'm glad,' she says. 'You've made a difference to us too. Especially Finn. I hope you know that. And you'll always be welcome here.'

I find Finn in the sitting room, engrossed at the laptop on Joy's desk. He looks round when I say hello: he doesn't seem the least bit surprised to see me.

'I've booked the hall for the first week in September,' he says, as if we've been mid-conversation all the while. 'So now we have to get everything together really quickly. Find a way to display the photographs. It's got to look professional.'

'It doesn't have to look slick,' I say. 'The whole point is that it's ordinary people, talking about what they love and value. It *should* look home-made. From the heart.'

'We've got to convince people first,' Finn says. 'They might not want anything to do with it.'

I think for a bit. 'Maybe it shouldn't look too political,' I say. 'Maybe the focus should be on celebrating and recording something real and important about the island. Maybe that's what would bring everyone on board. And that might be the most effective thing of all. People working together.'

'I'm seeing Isla this afternoon,' Finn says. 'I'm going to talk to her first of all.'

I smile, but I don't say anything. I draw up a chair, and we start looking at all the photos Finn's taken since I left him yesterday. A sequence of the sun setting behind the off-islands with layers of mist; sea breaking on to the sand in early morning light; sheep and half-grown lambs walking along the road above the Manse. A flock of lapwings taking off in flight above the loch; geese flying in a 'V' across a cloud-streaked sky; black and white oystercatchers standing in a row along the rocks, all facing the newly risen sun, like the morning after the party.

'You're a natural,' I say. 'These are gorgeous, Finn.'

He shows me his notes about people he wants to talk to. Not just the fishermen and crofters, but the people in the ferry office, and the shopworkers and postman and the café owner and the mechanic at the garage.

It really might work, I think. It's worth trying, at

least. It's good seeing how much energy Finn has for his new project.

'Where's everyone else?' I ask him. 'Your house seems really quiet.'

Finn shrugs. 'No idea. I think Jamie and Clara are packing up, ready to go back to London.'

Joy comes in, waving my list in her hand. 'All done. I've told everyone except Isla's dad who must still be out on the boat.'

'Thank you so much,' I say to Joy.

'You can tell Isla,' I say to Finn, 'when you see her later today.'

He nods.

Joy looks from Finn to me and back to Finn again, as if she's trying to understand something. But she doesn't say anything. She goes back out.

'What happened to Isla's mum?' I ask Finn. 'Has she got one? She's never mentioned her. There was no sign of anyone at the house that time I went there.'

'She left. She couldn't stand living here. She went back to Glasgow to live. Isla hardly ever sees her.' Finn shifts on his chair. 'She doesn't like to talk about it.'

'OK,' I say. 'Fair enough.'

Back at home, I start feeling – what is it, exactly? Not homesick, but something a bit like that. A creeping sense of the life going on here on the island being separate from me: the knowledge that I don't really belong here and never will. I'm just a visitor, passing through. And yet being here has touched me and changed me so much.

At bedtime, I stand for a moment in the other bedroom, where Bonnie will sleep when she finally gets here. The wind's rattling the skylight windows, shaking and buffeting the house, screeching down the chimney into the peat stove downstairs. Clouds scud across the moon. Bonnie will already be on her way from Spain, a long journey that will bring her steadily northwards. She'll have no idea how much things are changing every day, Mum and me getting closer together in a way we haven't been for ages.

Back in my own room, I get my diary out, ready to fill the next blank pages. They are filling up fast now. Hardly any left. The story of my heart. It's a story all about change, I realise now.

The moon's three-quarters full. For a moment the ragged strips of cloud clear completely and the moon shines directly on to my bed. It's such a strange and beautiful light. There's a single bright star – a planet, perhaps.

Sam would know. Sam, who has never been anywhere other than a city, where the night sky is never properly dark, where you can hardly see the stars and planets, and yet he'd know the name and I don't. What does that tell me about Sam?

My mind flips back to that long, horrible night: the accident, the aftermath, Dad shaking with rage and Mum crying silently as I answered the policewoman's questions.

'You are never to get into a car with him, never even *see* him again,' Dad said. 'You have to promise us that.'

But Dad didn't keep his promises, did he? To have and to hold. . . . Till death us do part. All that.

I lie in bed, unable to sleep, staring up at the square of black sky framed in the window, my mind churning. The wind gets stronger: the whole house rattles and creaks and sighs. There are other sounds caught up in the wind: screams and howls, the roar of pounding waves. It's as if the house itself is out at sea all night long.

Even as the day breaks, the storm's still raging.

Twenty–seven

The storm batters the island all of Friday. I don't mind really: we've got lots to do for the dinner. Mum and I spend the day cooking and cleaning and getting everything ready. We make smoked mackerel pâté with cream. We bake bread. We make tomato soup for the vegetarians. Mum cooks two huge pans of lamb casserole and another one with vegetables. I make chocolate mousse for dessert. The little fridge is stuffed full by the time we've finished. Just salads and baked potatoes to do tomorrow.

Mid-afternoon, Mum and I walk down to the ferry terminal to find out what's happening. The rain's lifted, but the sea's grey, the waves whipped into white peaks. Birds cry and drift, swept by the wind that scours and roars and won't let up. The road is empty. There are no cars or lorries queuing in the car park either. No one outside on the pier, not even the usual ferry men in yellow sou'westers and boots.

'The boat left the mainland this morning,' the woman in the ferry office says, when we go inside to ask. 'But it can't land at the island. Not with the wind and the swell, and the high tide.'

'So what will happen?' Mum asks.

'She'll go all the way back again,' the woman says. 'Try again tomorrow.'

Mum looks at me. 'We'd better phone Bonnie from the call box.'

'You can use the pay phone here, in the waiting room, if you like,' the woman says.

Mum finds Bonnie's number, counts out change for the phone.

I listen while Mum talks. Bonnie's voice sounds tinny and strange. 'No. Yes, really rough. Loads of people are being sick,' she tells Mum. 'But I'm OK.'

'We'll pay for you to stay overnight if needs be,' Mum says. 'Find yourself a nice bed and breakfast place. Don't worry about the money.'

I tug Mum's sleeve. 'Tell her Tim's on the same ferry as her.'

'Here, Bonnie. Kate wants a word.' She hands me the phone. 'You tell her.'

'Hi, Bonnie. You OK? Look out for a bloke on the ferry called Tim. Tall, six foot three or so. Dark hair. Very good-looking; early twenties. He'll be smartly dressed probably: something like a tweed jacket and jeans. Tell him who you are. He knows me. I've spoken about you too.'

Bonnie laughs. 'Whatever for?'

'He's nice. Good fun. You can hang out together for the long journey. He'll know a good place to stay. You can have dinner even –'

'I'm not going up to a complete stranger! Honestly, Kate. What's the matter with you? I'm fine, in any case. I've got my book . . .'

'It's what island people do,' I tell her. 'You know, be friendly and open. He won't mind at all. He'll be pleased. And he's not a stranger!'

'Are you OK?' Bonnie asks. 'You sound kind of different –'

The phone crackles as the signal breaks up. 'See you soon!' I shout, but the line's already dead. I put the receiver back. 'We got cut off,' I tell Mum.

'It's the weather,' the woman says. 'It does that all the time.'

'What time will the ferry arrive tomorrow?' Mum asks her.

'Three-ish. If it comes at all. Check the shipping forecast in the morning. There's only a fifty-fifty chance of it getting through even if the wind drops, because of the swell and the tide.'

'What'll we do if she can't get here tomorrow?' I ask Mum on the walk back.

'We'll have the dinner without her. We're not letting all that food go to waste!'

Back at the house, we light a fire in the peat stove. Mum reads, and I daydream. It seems like a very long afternoon, evening, night. The wind doesn't give up, not for a moment. It begins to get on my nerves.

Just as dawn breaks, the wind drops. When I wake properly, the sky is a clear blue, and the sun's shining on the sea, turning it a dazzling silver. The ferry will be leaving the mainland about now. I imagine Bonnie, beautiful with her tanned skin and blonde hair and open smiling face. Tim will surely have noticed her, even if she hasn't spoken to him yet . . . perhaps he'll offer her a lift up to the house when they arrive at the island, the way people do here . . .

But I want to be there to welcome her. I can't not be.

I pull on my jeans and jumper, run downstairs and stuff my boots on and open the front door wide. The sun's warm on my face, the air full of birdsong. It's the perfect day, everything bright and shiny. I'm absurdly happy, as if it's my island, and I want it to look its best for Bonnie, so she'll fall totally in love with it the moment she steps off the ferry.

Mum comes out of her bedroom and joins me on the doorstep, still in her nightie. 'Aren't we lucky?' she says. 'If it stays fine, we could even eat outside tonight, the first time all holiday! We can open out those French doors from the living room on to the patio and people can drift in and out.'

She puts her arms round me and hugs me close. 'I know it's silly, but I'm nervous about having so many new people here. You will help, won't you?'

'Of course I will. And you'll love Finn's family, honestly, Mum. Everyone's really friendly and fun.'

We eat our breakfast outside, even though it's only just warm enough. Mum pours our coffee into the hare cups. 'I'm going to buy a whole set before we go,' she says. 'A family of coffee cups. For the new house we're going to buy.'

I really don't want to think about that, but there's something touching about the way Mum's gathering herself together again, for the next stage of life without Dad. So I make an effort too. 'What kind of house?' I ask her.

'Something small, whatever I can afford I suppose. I'll have to increase my hours at work, get a mortgage again. But it'll be all right. Don't worry.'

'I can't wait to see Bonnie,' I say.

'Me too. I'm really excited,' Mum says. 'It's been three months. She'll look different: she's spent that whole time under the Spanish sun. She'll be brown as a berry!'

'Unlike us!'

'Yes. Though actually you look – kind of healthy.'

That makes me laugh. 'Mum! Is that the best you can do?'

'No, I mean, it suits you, all that time you've spent outside. You look better than you have done for ages, Kate. Healthy and bright-eyed. Happier, despite everything.'

The morning drags. Mum's all on edge, tidying everything even though it's already tidy. In the end I give up trying to be helpful and go outside. I find myself wandering through the village and up the hill. I check my phone but there's nothing from Sam. I try not to be disappointed.

Just as I'm setting off back down the road in the direction of the Manse I meet the jeep coming the other way. Piers is driving, Thea next to him. They slow down and stop.

Finn's in the back. He slides the window open. 'Hello, Kate!'

'Off walking again?' Piers teases.

'Not really. Where are you all going?'

'The beach, via Isla's. Picking her up on the way. Want to come?'

I hesitate.

'Do come,' Finn says. 'Please, Kate.'

'OK.'

I climb in the back next to Finn. He squeezes my hand. 'We're planning to swim,' he says. 'Want to stop off and get your stuff?'

I run into the house, grab my swimming things and run out again. Mum comes out to the jeep. 'Will you be back in time for Bonnie?'

'Of course.'

'Will you go straight there?'

'I don't know, Mum. I haven't thought yet. I'll come home first if there's time.'

'We're looking forward to the dinner this evening,' Thea says politely. 'Thank you so much for inviting us.'

Mum smiles. 'You're welcome,' she says. 'Have a lovely morning at the beach.'

Isla seems more friendly; she and Finn get on fine. I wonder briefly what happened when he went to see her yesterday. They are much more relaxed without Tim being there. They swim together, and Piers swims too.

Thea and I watch from the beach.

'I thought at one point that maybe you and Finn would get together . . .' Her voice trails off.

'Just friends,' I tell her. 'Lovely friends, but he's besotted with Isla. And now he's going to be staying here, something might actually happen.'

'Maybe,' Thea says. 'But Isla's quite ambitious. She'll be off to Glasgow soon as she's done her exams. And I'm not sure you're right about Finn's feelings.'

'Isla will be back, soon as she's finished her midwifery training.'

'Is that what she wants to do? I'd no idea.' Thea looks thoughtful. 'You know her better than I do.'

I lie on my stomach, sifting dry sand through my fingers. The breeze off the sea sends a shiver over my bare flesh, even though it's the middle of the day, the sun at its highest point.

'What do you think about Finn giving up school and his A levels?' Thea asks.

'I think it's wonderful. Totally the right thing for him.' I say the words so firmly there's no room for any further discussion. Even so, it's obvious Thea doesn't agree. But Piers is running up the beach now, dripping wet, his skin red and raw from the cold and she clicks into action. She finds his towel, organises his dry clothes, pours him tea from a flask.

'I'll give you a lift back if you like,' he says to me. 'Soon as I've got dressed. So you're not late for your sister.'

* * *

He drives fast, but I'm not bothered about the speed any more. It doesn't feel dangerous because I know how few cars there are, and how far ahead you can see. No sudden bends or corners.

'I'll drop you at your house,' he says. 'It's still too early for the ferry.'

'Do you think it will make it this time?'

'Depends on the mixture of swell and tide. Probably. Say hi to Tim, if he's there. Tell him we'll see him back at the Manse later this afternoon.'

Mum's filled the house with flowers: wild ones, picked from the fields. They're in jugs and jam jars all over the place, spilling pollen on to the clean surfaces of the windowsill and the table and the bookcase. Upstairs in Bonnie's room Mum's put a small posy of wild roses and grasses on the shelf next to the bed.

I wander into my own room. I pick up the blue-grey shell that Dad gave me, stroke my finger over the smooth mother-of-pearl inside. I put it back next to the pebble from Finn. I lie on my bed to write some more of my diary.

'Ready?' Mum calls up. 'Time to go.'

We walk fast.

'Look!' I point. The ferry's coming along the bay, hugging the coast, almost here. As we watch, it slows down and begins to turn. We can hear the roar of the engine as it manoeuvres ready for docking.

We break into a half-run. Cars and cattle trucks are queuing in the car park: two days' worth of traffic. We join the small line of foot passengers. Already, the ferry's reversing, ready to tie up, and up on deck I can see Bonnie, waving madly. And she does look amazing, just as we imagined, Mum and I.

We're waving, and staring, and my heart does a funny leap, because Bonnie isn't alone. Next to her, hair pinned up so she looks older and much more sophisticated, is Hannah!

Mum gives a little cry, and rushes forwards. She looks as if she is about to sob her heart out. The ferry bloke makes her wait, to let the cars off first. But Bonnie and Hannah are already running down the gangplank, and hugging Mum, and as I catch up they hug me too.

'My girls!' Mum says, over and over. 'My three gorgeous girls, safe and here all together.'

In all the rush and excitement I forget about Tim. He must have driven past without us noticing. We walk back to the house, everyone talking at once, and Bonnie and Hannah saying how beautiful it is and remembering things from when they were little, and all of us laughing when Hannah drags her case on wheels through a big dollop of sheep poo.

'There it is,' Mum says as we cross over the cattle grid past the shop. 'The small white house on the right with the big window.'

I help Hannah tug her case over the grass and Mum helps Bonnie with her bag. There's so much laughter and talking as we go inside and they dump their stuff and then suddenly, for a moment, we all go quiet at the same time.

The sense of someone missing is overwhelming.

Four of us, instead of five.

Mum smiles bravely. We're all so obviously thinking the same thing.

Bonnie breaks the spell. 'Dad's an idiot,' she says.

'His loss,' Hannah says.

'We're going to be fine,' Mum says firmly. 'We'll miss him like mad, but we will be all right. I promise you.'

The weather's changing by the minute. Clouds, sun, the wind picking up, singing along the telephone wires and sending white clouds of thistledown over the grass. It's too cold to sit outside for long so we set the table in the living room. Hannah polishes the wine glasses with a cloth, fills jugs with water while Bonnie and I make the salad. Mum opens a bottle of wine and pours a glass for Hannah and herself.

'Does everything look OK?' Mum keeps asking.

'It's all fine,' Hannah says. 'It doesn't matter what it looks like, in any case.'

Joy and Alex and everyone from the Manse, except Finn, arrives bang on time, and as soon as they are all talking and laughing and pouring drinks I relax completely. Alex makes a point of looking after Mum: he's courteous and gentlemanly in a way that delights her and makes her sparkle. *Almost* flirting.

'Go, Mum,' Hannah says, watching them.

'That's Alex!' I tell her. 'Married to Joy. Married for *ever.*'

Tim's talking to Bonnie, of course. They did meet on the ferry. *He*'s being charming too. He listens to her talking about the farm in Spain where she's been working, and about her plans to do some sort of environmental work next year. Hannah thinks she remembers Piers and Jamie from when they were little and played together on the beach. She and Thea and Jamie talk about living in London.

Finn finally turns up. He hands me Dad's camera. 'You could take some pictures tonight,' he says.

I hang the camera in the lobby and wander after Finn. I introduce him to my sisters, and he tells them about the wind farm almost immediately. Bonnie has lots to say about it, being Bonnie. She explains why it's so expensive having offshore wind turbines – maintaining and operating them, sub-sea cables and stuff, which is why the operating companies prefer the option closer to land . . . and that gets Mackie and the man from the café heated up, talking loudly about disruptions to *fishing* and birds . . .

I watch Finn's face light up as he tells them about the great northern divers, and the special protected status, and our plans to fight back. Tim joins in: he says he can imagine a fantastic island broadcast project about listening to the sounds of the Hebrides. *It's really going to happen*, I think. *And I'm a tiny part of it too. Standing up for something good. Making a difference.*

I help Mum get the casseroles and potatoes out of the oven, just as Isla turns up with her dad. Fiona arrives soon after, her arms full of bottles of champagne. 'Never seen so many people in this room before!' she tells Mum, who immediately starts apologising.

'Stop that!' Fiona says. 'It's a lovely thing to bring

people together. And what a wonderful spread.' She knows most people already, of course, but she's surprised that we have made so many friends this summer.

Just as it's beginning to get dark, I wander out through the French doors on to the little garden at the side of the house.

Bonnie follows me outside. 'Let's light the candles,' she says. One by one she lights the candles in the small coloured glasses which we arranged earlier in a line down the centre of the wooden garden table.

'So pretty,' she says. She turns and hugs me suddenly. 'Oh, Kate! It must have been awful for you, all alone with Mum and Dad, and all this stuff going on.'

'Horrible,' I say. 'Yes, but not all the time. There have been amazing things happening. I've met all these lovely people. I've fallen in love with the island. We're going to come back to this house next summer, Mum and me. You and Hannah should come too.'

'Do you think they'll get back together again?' Bonnie asks. 'Won't Dad realise he's made a terrible mistake?'

'I don't know,' I say. 'I don't understand any of it. I guess it's too complicated. And they don't tell us what's really going on.'

I tell her about the wild geese poem that Dad recited to me, our first day on the island. 'I think he was telling me how lonely he felt,' I say. 'But I still don't understand why.'

Bonnie's quiet for ages. The candles flicker, but they stay alight. The sky over the sea has turned an extraordinary colour: dark turquoise fading into green, and as the sun goes down it throws its path of gold across the water. The light changes all the time. The sun sinks behind the islands and the blue-green of the sky deepens and darkens to navy and blue-black. We see the first stars appear.

'And are you really all right?' Bonnie asks.

I nod.

'That boy's nice. Finn.'

I smile.

'He watches you,' Bonnie says. 'He likes you, I can tell.'

'Oh, Bonnie!' I say. 'Not you too. We're friends. There's someone else he likes more.'

Bonnie makes a funny *hmmm* sound, as if she isn't convinced. 'Well,' she says. 'It's the best way to start, as *friends*, in any case. It's much more likely to work out, if you know each other really well first.'

Hannah opens the French doors. 'Come back in and be sociable, you two,' she calls. 'Food's ready.'

Bonnie goes to join her.

I walk round the outside of the house and in through the front door to pick up Dad's camera from the coat hook. I go back out through the gate, over the grass, across the road and down on to the beach.

The tide's going down. I perch the camera on a rock to keep it steady, and I take a whole sequence of photographs of the starlit sky. The bright planet. The rising moon.

I imagine sending the pictures to Sam: *this is what it was like.*

I turn my back to the sea to look up at the white square of the house, the windows all lit up, the shadows of people as they move round the rooms, and the light from the candles flickering in the garden. How warm and inviting it looks: our house full of friends, family, conversation. It's exactly how a house should be.

The sound of voices drifts over, carried on the wind, and mixes with the rasp of waves rolling shingle and the cry of seabirds flying low across the water to their roost on the black rocks.

Here we all are, on this small blue planet as it slowly turns, spinning through space, infinitely precious.

Q&A with the author

When you were Kate's age, what kind of books did you like to read?

When I was Kate's age, I was reading all the time, and moving between novels written for young people, like the *Flambards* series by K.M. Peyton and *The Owl Service* by Alan Garner, and the books we were reading at school: *Romeo and Juliet* and *Measure for Measure* by Shakespeare; *To Kill a Mockingbird* by Harper Lee; novels by Thomas Hardy (*Tess of the d'Urbervilles, Far from the Madding Crowd*) and D.H. Lawrence (*Sons and Lovers*). I read *Wuthering Heights* by Emily Brontë, *Jane Eyre* by Charlotte Brontë, and *Pride and Prejudice* by Jane Austen. I loved poetry too. I started reading the Romantic poets about this time (Keats, Wordsworth) and also poetry by Edward Thomas, Wilfred Owen, Dylan Thomas, Stevie Smith, Philip Larkin, Ted Hughes and Seamus Heaney. I loved Dodie Smith's *I Capture the Castle*; J.D. Salinger's *The Catcher in the Rye* and historical romances by Georgette Heyer and Jean Plaidy . . . I read widely, everything I could get my hands on! My parents love books and our family house was full of them.

When you are writing, to what extent do you draw on your own experiences?

All my stories are a mixture of 'real life', closely observed or remembered, and imagination. Memories, thoughts and feelings are transformed in the writing of them. But that's not the same as saying my novels are autobiographical. They most definitely are not! My characters are not me. They are all imagined, created by me. But I need to feel a connection to the material I am writing.

How long does it take you to write a book?

Different novels take different amounts of time. I think and dream and imagine and write notes for a long while before I start writing down the story. Once I know enough to start typing on my laptop, it takes me about nine months to a year. I'm a slow writer because I rewrite and edit a lot. Plus I'm not writing full-time: I have another job, as Senior Lecturer in Creative Writing at Bath Spa University.

If you could recommend just one book for everyone to read what would it be?

Impossible question, but it would have to be a children's book: *Tom's Midnight Garden* by Philippa Pearce. Like the best children's books, it's a book for readers of any age. It's a beautiful and moving story. It's perfectly constructed, I think, and profound about the connections between the young and the old, between past and present, and the importance of memory.

Why I wrote This Northern Sky

Some of the events in the novel are based on an amazing summer I spent in the Outer Hebrides when I was in my early twenties. We visited the most beautiful beaches I've ever seen. One night we camped and partied at a beach and saw the Northern Lights. Last year I went back to the Western Isles to research life on a different island, and those experiences helped me write Kate's story. The island in *This Northern Sky* is an imaginative recreation, rather than a particular one.

This is a novel about change and loss, as well as about growing up. I wanted to explore the complex feelings when parents split up, or are on the verge of doing so, from the viewpoint of a teenager caught in the middle, who has very little power over what happens but who is inevitably deeply affected by it.

The setting of the novel is not simply the place where events happen: it is intimately connected to the themes of the story. When Kate first arrives on the island, she sees it as a bleak place, with nothing and no one of interest. Gradually she learns about the island and the people who live there. As she begins to make new friends, she also starts to appreciate the raw beauty of the place, and see how a community of people can help and support each other. That's an important thing for her to learn at a time when her own family seems to be falling apart. I wanted to show how the natural world can be healing: I know that I am restored and helped by spending time outside, in wild, remote places where you are at the mercy of the weather and the sea and the rhythm of the tides. It gives you a different perspective on what's important. That's what I show happening to Kate, little by little. Although Kate can't stop her parents splitting up, she can find ways to take charge of her own life and find strength and hope in her relationships with other people.

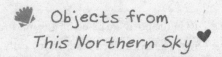

Objects from *This Northern Sky*

This is a novel of key images and sounds as well as 'objects': the story opens with an image of planet Earth viewed from space. The American astronomer and scientist Carl Sagan called it the 'pale blue dot': it is utterly beautiful and moving. It puts our lives into a different perspective and makes life on Earth seem infinitely precious.

Living on a remote island teaches you how dependent you are on the natural world of wind, tides and weather. I couldn't

This Northern Sky